MW01377958

WHAT BOOKS PRESS
AN IMPRINT OF
THE GLASS TABLE
COLLECTIVE
LOS ANGELES

ALSO BY A.W. DEANNUNTIS

Master Siger's Dream
The Mermaid at the Americana Arms Motel
The Final Death of Rock-and-Roll and Other Stories

THE MYSTERIOUS ISLANDS

AND OTHER STORIES

A.W. DEANNUNTIS

LOS ANGELES

Acknowledgement

The author offers thanks to the editors of the web-journal *Mobius* and the journal *Short Stories Bimonthly* for their publication of stories included in this collection.

Publisher's Cataloging-In-Publication Data

Names: DeAnnuntis, A. W. (Anthony W.).

Title: The mysterious islands and other stories / A.W. DeAnnuntis.

Description: Los Angeles : What Books Press, [2016]

Identifiers: ISBN 978-0-9962276-3-6

Subjects: LCSH: Islands--Fiction. | Magic--Fiction. | Sailors--Fiction. | Short stories, American.

Classification: LCC PS3604.E17 A6 2016 | DDC 813/.6--dc23

What Books Press
363 South Topanga Canyon Boulevard
Topanga, CA 90290

WHATBOOKSPRESS.COM

Cover art: Gronk, untitled, mixed media on paper, 2015.
Book design by Ash Goodwin, AshGood.com.

THE MYSTERIOUS ISLANDS

AND OTHER STORIES

for Gail

CONTENTS

THE MYSTERIOUS ISLANDS

Island of Doubt 15

Island of Glowing Towers 25

Island Of The Disappearing Cavern 35

Island Of The Lost Sailor 46

Island Of Golden Eyes 57

Island Of Sleepless Ghosts 67

Island Of Wandering Shadows 78

Island Of False Dreams 88

Island Of Stone Women 99

OTHER STORIES

Martin and the Dead Cats 111

I Shot JFK, Too 122

Ed Dreams Of Paris And Shoes 130

Waiting for the Widow 141

Brian's Unemployment Monkey 151

The Visitation 161

THE MYSTERIOUS ISLANDS

ISLAND OF DOUBT

AS PICTURED ON OUR MAP, the island's outline resembled a crescent whose northern end was broad but then narrowed until it formed a teardrop near its southern tip. We had journeyed there hopeful of uncovering artifacts at both locations. Accounts from past visitors also suggested possible remains of walls and foundations. But in addition, we hoped our research would lay to rest a peculiar myth concerning the island's inhabitants. We began our voyage optimistic and determined to add flesh to those speculative bones. We were confident our effort would result in knowledge.

Our ship dropped anchor close to the southern end of that bay formed by the island's crescent. Treeless and barren of features, the island was a nearly flat figure of yellow sand brilliant and enticing under the sun. Back at the institute we had assumed powerful sea currents along with strong prevailing winds gave the island its distinctive shape. We planned to trench both sites since neither was recorded as ever having been investigated. Thus, by the time we dropped anchor we were certain of what we should do and what we could hope to find. All of us except Henry.

Our team did not include anyone who had visited the island in the past so we carried a catalog of those few fragmentary artifacts recovered on previous visits. But earlier visitors had also described certain anomalous conditions on the island. Accounts varied but we were confident these could not be merely the result of unfamiliarity with conditions specific to the island. So as the evening of our arrival descended, we knew there were complications to our journey and their resolution would demand effort. And then Henry disappeared.

We did not discover his absence until the morning and so we assumed that late in the night he had somehow eluded the Captain's watch though we did not yet speculate on his reason. Since neither of our longboats was missing we were forced to assume he swam to the island though it lay a good distance from where we were anchored. But all this seemed so unlikely that our confusion was complete. Henry was simply our epigrapher, after all, had never visited this island before and had not appeared especially excited by this voyage. So his flight to the island under the cover of darkness seemed worse than unlikely and more than dangerous. But by this, our visit suddenly became burdened with a more urgent purpose. Whatever else we accomplished, we needed to find Henry.

Our Captain offered an inspired suggestion; assume he had swum from our ship, by rowing a longboat to follow the beach we should recognize any footprints left in the sand as he stepped from the surf. So as four sailors from our ship's crew rowed, we stared from the longboat across the water determined to see something useful. Yet under that fierce sun and against the brilliant sand every shadowed hollow resembled a footprint. Perhaps it was the result of visual exhaustion, but gradually discouragement set in until finally we rowed in silence, convinced his recovery would prove difficult if it was successful at all.

Then, near midday we recognized beyond the edge of the surf a cluster of indentations that resembled footprints. But we were startled to suspect they appeared to have been made by more than one person. We had been confident the island was uninhabited and we had detected no signs of human presence. Thus, even before landing we had acquired another mystery.

Urging us all to be cautious the Captain beached our boat and we clambered out.

Reaching the cluster of marks in the sand, immediately we began to speculate. A single line of marks of different sizes appeared at the edge of the surf as if emerging from the sea and continued in a straight line. Just above the waterline it seemed that whoever had made these marks then had hesitated and perhaps looked around to orient himself. Because of this we were convinced most of these marks had been made by Henry, but apparently not all. The non-Henry marks were broad and short and appeared deeper than those we assumed were his. But most baffling, all of the footprints appeared to stop a short distance from the surf. We each moved off in a different direction suspecting the constant wind had disguised the rest of these marks and that they resumed being visible a short distance away.

Although we followed the island's bald undulating mounds of scintillating and shifting sand, under that piercing sun we failed to find additional marks and this alarmed us. Several of us were determined to continue the search but our Captain concluded that, considering the heat, it was better that we return to the ship for rest and a meal and to plot our next step.

Back on board the ship our conviction grew that despite Henry's disappearance we needed to begin those excavations which had brought us here. Besides, it seemed inevitable that on such a barren island, eventually he must be found. There was, after all, no other place for him to go.

Originally our plan had been to complete a trench at the southern site before beginning excavation of the northern. It now seemed urgent to retrieve and document what we could in anticipation of Henry's return. His disappearance certainly was disheartening, but recognition of additional footprints left the uncomfortable suggestion that strangers were visiting the island and this added disturbing urgency to every plan for what we hoped to effect. In the end we agreed that having anchored near the southern site, early the next day we would begin to excavate there.

Despite Henry's disappearance we remained eager to begin, so night found each of us restless. The following day would begin early and promised to be one of strenuous effort, yet on deck there was much pacing and muttered conversation. And while our work was the overt topic, speculation over what had happened to Henry and who else might be on the island was at the back of each of our minds. And then we saw the fire.

Because it was a moonless night and the terrain featureless, we could not decide whether it was a small fire nearby or a large fire at some distance. Despite this confusion, several among us insisted they saw a silhouette pass back and forth before that fire and speculated that it was Henry's and he was attempting to signal to us. But what most baffled us was where whoever had built that fire had found sufficient wood to fuel it. We had seen scraps of wood scattered along the edge of the surf but there seemed hardly enough to build even a small cooking fire. Several of us urged the Captain to sail to a spot near the fire so we could observe it, but he insisted that at night and in unfamiliar waters such an excursion was dangerous and that besides, sunrise would provide us all of the information we could need.

In our research preparatory to our voyage we encountered a peculiar myth involving the island which had been recorded on a neighboring but distant island. That legend asserted the island's inhabitants worshiped creatures from the sky who had physical congress with them which resulted in offspring. These offspring, when they reached a particular age, then disappeared into the sea swimming off dolphin-like never to be seen again.

As unlikely as all of that seemed, we were determined to excavate any corroborating evidence, particularly inscriptions; thus the importance of Henry's participation. Legends, after all, always spring from some historical event or moment and it was that reality which we were determined to recover.

Several additional parts of the legend contributed peculiar elements. One was that the inhabitants of the island could signal a request for the visitors' appearance and the visitors would respond, and according to the legend, these creatures instantly were able to resolve every problem. Unfortunately the legend did not describe how this signaling was accomplished, and this was something we hoped to reveal. A related element of the legend was that the islanders had no written language, and so had adopted the language of the alien visitors. This last was the reason Henry had been invited to join our team. We hoped to associate any language fragments uncovered to some terrestrial language and so identify what remained as non-terrestrial. Finally, the legend alleged that the visitors would transport these islanders in their vehicles wherever they wished to go. This was particularly intriguing since residents of a distant island claimed common ancestry insisting they had reached their island by way of these visitors' vehicles. So we had arrived optimistic that whatever truth these legends possessed would be confirmed by material evidence. But now, under their influence, sight of this fire stimulated a distracting license to our speculations. For all of these reason we became impatient to return to the island and examine the remains of that fire.

Sunrise was nearly upon us when our longboat returned to the beach, although the air was already hot and threatened to be brutal by midday.

We had planned to begin a full-scale excavation that day and so we carried a variety of tools. On landing we headed to the site of the fire watching for anything that might offer evidence of who had made it. Drawing close, we saw many more footprints than we had expected but each was distorted by its neighbor so that, clustered in such a small area they suggested nothing. Finally standing over its remains, we were surprised by how large the fire had been.

But we were confused that we found no fragments of it beyond its irregular circle of blackened sand. No bits of partially burned straw or pieces of charred logs; nothing but blackened sand filled the center of its circle. Baffled and no longer certain of what we were seeing we decided to dig.

And to our confusion, the fire-blackened sand continued down much deeper than we expected. We dug until our pit was more than two yards deep but the sand remained black and the width of the fire did not narrow. None of us could think of a way to account for the intensity of the heat which this suggested; it appeared as if the fire's flames had somehow vented directly from beneath the island's sand. But at this depth the dry sand had become unstable and the pit now was dangerous.

Our equipment included a canvas we planned to suspend over our excavation to shield us from the sun. We assembled its shelter and huddled under it to eat a quick meal and exchange large portions of speculation. Foremost remained the question of what could have happened to Henry. We assumed at least some of those footprints had been left by him. But we found none beyond those encircling the fire, either approaching or retreating. Someone laughingly suggested they had been made by those legendary visitors who had descended from the sky while we were distracted by the fire and had then taken Henry with them.

Two hours past midday, a breeze sprang up from the south to moderate the heat. We returned to the site and began a shallow trench to test our assumptions.

A few inches below the surface we struck a stone. To that point we had found nothing on the island larger than pebbles and sand, so this discovery left us perplexed. We moved aside enough sand to expose marks on the stone that appeared incised and which resembled some form of writing. But we could only speculate; none of us recognized this lettering or its language. Hardly a day into our visit we had found a particular need for Henry's assistance. We decided to expose the context of this stone.

Digging just a foot further down, we uncovered another piece of stone also inscribed with marks and these resembled those of the first. But most oddly, the two stones were otherwise unconnected. The upper had not been stacked immediately atop the lower stone but was skewed to one side. And more problematically, there were several inches of loose sand between them as if the lower had been covered over before the upper was placed over it, and this struck all of us as more than unlikely. But worse, we could not recognize where these stones could have come from. We had been led to expect remains of foundations, but we had uncovered no naturally-occurring stone on the island so these stones had to have been imported to the island, and we could not imagine why. Digging further, we found that below these was only more loose sand. Confronted by the inscrutable, we decided to begin a second trench and perhaps recognize some purpose or intention.

Excavation of that trench demanded nearly the rest of the day but we found only sand and as far down as we dug. Sunset approached and exhausted, hungry and frustrated, we returned to the longboat and to our ship. We did not speak of our disappointment.

Our evening meal was again dominated by wildly restless speculation. After our meal we returned to the deck looking for a refreshing breeze. Amid the canopy of stars overhead we were startled by what we assumed were two stars seeming to move slowly toward each other until they appeared to converge, slightly bobbing and dancing a small distance apart. This left us speechless because it was beyond every reasonable speculation. After some minutes and just as suddenly, these two lights separated and moved off rapidly in different directions before winking out.

After a long and confused silence one of us offered the only suggestion that had not been spoken; we had just witnessed the rendezvous of two space vehicles. The fact that this speculation coincided with the legend triggered an unfocused but urgent concern for ourselves. We would not admit what more we suspected, but an alternative explanation eluded us. And then we saw the second fire.

Although we could not be certain, this fire appeared to be burning at the same spot as that of the previous night. But that deep pit we had dug there earlier in the day had not been filled in. This fire appeared to be burning at the surface of the sand, and not obscured within that hole we had left. Again we appealed to the Captain to bring our ship close enough for us to gain a clear view of this fire. And once again he refused, although he offered one of the longboats to anyone sufficiently intrepid to make the excursion. In the end four of us agreed to travel to the island while the rest watched from the ship.

For those of us remaining on the ship, the crew of the longboat appeared to make rapid progress across the lagoon, but a short distance from the beach it suddenly stopped. Some moments passed before we realized the crew continued to row but the boat remained fixed as if frozen in the water.

We called out asking what had happened, but the distance to the longboat muted our voices. Our ship carried a second longboat and we asked the Captain for its use but he refused insisting he could not afford to lose both boats. The crew of the longboat finally gave up and returned to our ship. When asked, each claimed that it was as if an invisible hand had closed around them. We turned to the Captain as if this was something he understood but he admitted he was as baffled as any of us. Confined to the rail, every eye fixed on that fire as if one of us was about to recognize something obscure to the rest.

The fire suddenly bloomed to grow very large and then silhouettes of several figures appeared before it and moving back and forth. Our distance was too great to discern their number, let alone what they were doing, but their actions suggested agitation. We attempted to conjure a hypothesis to account for what we saw. The wind suddenly died and we discovered that a sound seemed to emanate from the direction of the fire.

Low in pitch and volume, this sound more resembled a hum. It gradually grew louder and although it lacked any discernible characteristic, we were certain it was intentional. The agitation of the silhouettes increased with changes in the sound and then we became frightened.

Our fear though urgent was oddly unfocused and it washed over us in waves. Nothing in the gestures of the agitated figures seemed related to the sound. And more perplexing, each of us became certain the sound was somehow directed uniquely for them; some voice determined to speak directly to that person. And each of us assumed responsibility for deciphering this message since the fate of our ship and our lives appeared exclusively theirs. Guilt and that responsibility we each assumed drove us deeper into ourselves making consultation impossible. We paced the deck withdrawn and pondering.

Gradually that sound became less a noise than a pressure building inside the skull and grew until it caused some of us to hallucinate. Our hallucinations varied; some were of recognizable figures or creatures, while others were abstract and failed description. But we endured an anxiety unmatched by anything we had yet experienced. So it demanded a moment to recognize that what we experienced was guilt and responsibility toward Henry.

He had not been a popular member of our expedition. Few of us had worked with him and none expressed personal loyalty to him. Even the Captain's concern for Henry's fate was an abstract responsibility for the welfare of one of his passengers. But perhaps finally we recognized that we had abandoned a colleague in distress in order to pursue a higher priority.

And worse, that abandonment had been spontaneous and without hesitation. Having lost Henry, we had all simply moved on to what needed to be done for the success of the expedition. Even our Captain came to suspect something profound had reshaped our expedition into a different enterprise. But this recognition did not suggest what we needed to do next.

Staring across the lagoon to watch the fire, we struggled against a sort of lethargy creeping over us. Without a clear path to follow, each of us struggled within a swamp of baffling and unresolved possibilities.

The fire grew still larger as that low, throbbing sensation became stronger within our heads. Someone suggested that either we block our ears or return to the island. But just as suddenly as the sound had arisen, it stopped. Several of us feared having gone deaf, the cessation of the sound was that abrupt. Our attention returned to the fire since it and the sound seemed related. We assumed we should now recognize a change in the fire, but it neither grew nor diminished. Confused, we could only watch its tongues of golden flame lick the black sky.

But our thoughts returned to Henry. Was there some connection between the fire and his disappearance? Was he in danger and in need of rescue? Could his disappearance have been voluntary? After all, he had fled our ship and left no evidence of abduction. Could he have been lured or even coerced to leave our ship but then hid himself somehow on that flat and featureless spot of land?

We recognized then that we were asking more questions about Henry than we had when he first disappeared. And then, just as suddenly as it had appeared, the fire went out.

Our discussion of Henry had so dominated our attention that we had left off watching the fire. With the fire gone, those silhouettes disappeared as well, but had whatever had cast them also gone? Again it seemed urgent that we return to the island to investigate. We appealed to the Captain and this time he approved. He recognized that if we waited until morning our questions would not be answered. He assigned the first-mate to lead a crew to the island.

Several of us volunteered and the longboat was quickly launched. To our surprise, we reached the beach this time without incident. In the darkness we could only guess the location of the fire. The beams of our lanterns bounced over the yellow sand like drunken fireflies as we spread out determined to locate footprints we could follow. After some wandering we decided this strategy was not yielding results. We assumed we had been moving in the general direction of the fire but we were unable even to find that hole we had excavated earlier.

Like our cleverest speculations, our wandering over the island yielded nothing. Finally we returned to the longboat. Perhaps in response to our gloomy expressions the first-mate suggested that this was the reason the silhouette figures had permitted us to land; we would only be allowed to investigate when there was nothing left to be discovered.

Back on board we reported our failure to the Captain. He paused but said nothing before he turned and walked away, as if this was all as he had expected.

Our failure left us frustrated and so even more restless. Speculation continued but exhaustion finally drove us to our bunks and to agitated sleep. And perhaps our exhaustion had been deeper than we had anticipated. Even the Captain's watch must have been overcome, because it was far into the morning before an alarm was sounded. An enormous storm of high winds and gigantic waves was raging; a storm of such power that stepping onto the deck risked being washed instantly overboard. With the hatches sealed and equipment tied down, we prepared to ride out this storm.

Or we believed ourselves prepared. Because late in the day the storm became worse. The wind howled through the rigging as tremendous waves that beat against our sides washed over the deck. And then, early in the evening, leaks began to appear. Our research team was drafted to help man the pumps and it was all we could do to remain afloat. The storm drove our ship to drag against its anchor with such force the Captain ordered additional anchors set. But before that could be done the anchor cable snapped and then our danger grew worse; we floundered at the mercy of the storm.

The Captain ordered his crew to set a replacement anchor, but even the most experienced sailors were battered by the storm's fury. The Captain had no choice except to keep the ship headed into the wind even while that wind continued to shift. The first-mate nearly lost his life struggling at the helm. Helpless before the power of this storm we were compelled simply to wait.

As best as we could judge, nearly twenty-four hours passed before the storm finally began to subside. When it weakened sufficiently, the Captain ordered his crew on-deck to reset the anchor and this time they succeeded. But it was not until late the following day that the rest of us were able to step out onto the deck to survey the damage, and that damage proved worse than we had imagined.

Ropes and cables of the rigging rested on the deck as an enormous knot. Several of our sails hung ripped and shredded like deflated balloons. One of the yards and one of the spars lay shattered on the deck. And worst, both longboats had their sides stove in and were now useless for anything more than firewood. This survey demanded some time and no one thought of anything else. But finally, someone asked what had happened to the island.

At first the Captain assumed the storm had driven us far off course, so as soon as the clouds parted and he had a clear view of the sky he took readings. To our surprise, despite the storm's violence we were less than twenty miles from our original position. We were hardly seaworthy and he ordered repairs sufficient to return us to port. But we reminded him that despite the storm we had to assume Henry remained somewhere on the island and we needed to find him. Although concerned for the condition of his ship, he agreed to make one more attempt to find Henry.

We sailed to our original coordinates but several moments passed before we began to suspect the island was gone. At first we wondered if the Captain's readings had been mistaken so we continued to sail. But eventually we recognized that the island had disappeared, leaving not even a ripple on the ocean's surface. We were so stunned we could not speak to each other. Finally the Captain suggested that at low tide at least the remnants of the island should become visible, and so we lingered, determined to remain optimistic. But at the hour of low tide the surface remained unbroken. None of us seemed to have a useful suggestion to offer but it was clear we had no alternative; the Captain ordered his crew to sail for port and we could offer no reasonable objection.

As our ship began to move we stood beside the rail and looked to where we believed we had seen that island. Had Henry still been beside us we might even have doubted our island had ever existed. But he was not and now he never would be. We sailed for home doubtful of all we had witnessed and compelled to embrace that doubt and all that it failed to contain.

ISLAND OF GLOWING TOWERS

THE ISLAND'S FOREST of stone towers resembled multicolored smokestacks, and the four antique photographs of these imposing structures which we had consulted promised a visually compelling excursion. Assumed the product of springs flowing beneath the surface of the island in combination with erosion of wind and water, the suspicion remained that humans had been involved with their appearance. We expected to answer questions concerning these towers along with any involvement humans may have had.

Our Captain was an elderly man nearing retirement and ours would be his last voyage. Although sentimentally charming, this assured us that ours would be a cautious journey, and for this we were relieved. In addition to a chemist, a geologist, a hydrologist, a meteorologist and a medical doctor, late in our preparations we added an astronomer to our team. She planned to make observations crucial to her study of asteroids and comets and we were pleased to help a fellow-scientist even if she was an astronomer.

In addition, on the possibility that human remains were discovered we also included a well-known anthropologist recently awarded an important prize and also, like our Captain, nearing retirement. Considering the distance separating this island from its neighbors it seemed unlikely to provide such evidence, so if any was uncovered it would be significant.

We sailed into the island's small bay shortly after mid-day to enjoy our first glimpse of its exotic terrain, and even before our ship dropped anchor we were eager to disembark. But our Captain cautioned us that twilight fell quickly at this latitude, and with erratic currents swirling about the island such a visit involved unnecessary risk. Several of us expressed frustration that he was being overly-cautious but in the end we agreed to his decision.

Our astronomer, however, was particularly annoyed by our Captain's decision. She complained bluntly that she should be permitted at least to position her instruments on the island, insisting this could be done quickly and without risk. But having voiced her complaint she resigned herself to his decision.

However and to our surprise, our anthropologist was also emphatic in his disapproval of the Captain's decision. He had been quiet during our voyage keeping mostly to himself so even the Captain was startled by his vehemence. When challenged, he emphasized the difference between the practice of his own discipline and that of our astronomer's, insisting the shackles imposed by our studies should not hamper her. Although a weak argument, he appeared determined to support her and any rationale was sufficient. Several of us privately confessed the hope no human remains would be found since it seemed unlikely he would find the inclination to record and study them. Our astronomer, meanwhile, appeared oddly uncomfortable about his enthusiasm. Flattered perhaps by this older scientist's attention she seemed embarrassed by his fervor. The rest of us were perplexed at how all of this might resolve but we found ourselves curious to see how it did.

At the end of that first day we took our meal at the Captain's table and afterward, caressed by a sweet-smelling darkness we strolled about the deck. Our astronomer moved to the quarter-deck beside the wheel where she used her devices to make a series of sightings. Later our Captain joined us on-deck and then made his way to the wheel where he had a brief conversation with her. None of us overheard their discussion but our anthropologist seemed especially curious.

Sunrise found all of us awake early and eager to depart. But as we gathered for breakfast our anthropologist seemed ill at-ease and when we stood to travel to the island he demurred stating that he had not slept well and there were notes he needed to review. As we departed he reminded us that if human remains were suspected we should preserve them undisturbed.

From the deck of our ship that forest of stone towers at sunrise provided a marvelous vision of sparkling and shimmering colors, but when finally we stood beneath and among them its experience was astonishing. Stacked like stone pancakes, the startling color of each layer clearly distinguished it from those above and below. Our geologist speculated that the chemical composition of each provided unique data about the island's conditions at the time that layer formed. As exciting as it was to move among these towers, our geologist reminded us to be cautious and assume they were not stable. As evidence, many of the stacks displayed cracks and several had collapsed, their fragments scattered as shards of colorful rubble that resembled crystal confetti.

Our geologist assumed that hot springs emerging from below the surface must supply the material for these towers, and pointed out indications of the way wind and occasional earthquakes had modified their shape. Assuming the role of photographer, she assured us her photographs would be valuable since if a layer collapsed its evidence would not be lost. She then reminded us that this should assure us the island itself must be unstable. Standing among those towers and recognizing the subtle variations in their shapes and hues, we looked for signs that might suggest human involvement and thereby provide our anthropologist the opportunity to demonstrate he was as useful as he was annoying.

Our astronomer meanwhile turned out to be a capable and enthusiastic assistant. Since her research could only be conducted after nightfall, once she had positioned her instruments she seemed eager to help the rest of us. Our research suggested the island was uninhabited and so we assumed that left behind her equipment would remain undisturbed. After a long day exploring different quadrants of the island under a blistering sun, we returned to our ship.

Our Captain presided over our evening meal at his table inviting each of us to describe what we had seen and what we had accomplished along with our expectations for the following day. Oddly our anthropologist joined him in asking questions. Although he had spent that day aboard ship he appeared as curious as our Captain about our observations.

We were a friendly group and shared our experiences and our thoughts with casual good-humor. When our astronomer described her plan for later that evening however, our anthropologist's face took on a pained expression before he offered his help. His concern startled us, but our astronomer simply smiled with confused embarrassment before thanking him for his offer.

With our meal finished the Captain instructed two of his sailors to row our astronomer to the island and then remain to provide any help she needed before returning her to our ship. None of us were surprised when our anthropologist repeated his offer of help, and he appeared disappointed when again she declined.

While their longboat headed into the darkness toward the island several of us remained on-deck to watch its progress. Aided by the light from a quarter-moon, we managed to follow the longboat until it beached and then watched the lanterns of the group move like bright dots floating over a velvet background. From our distance the sight of their lights moving within that forest of sparkling and refracting stone towers left us startled. Their crystalline surfaces scattered those lantern's light in star-like patterns then reflected by adjacent towers as glowing echoes which then passed from tower to tower. After some time following the group's movements, to our surprise one lantern left the group and quickly returned to the beach. Then to our astonishment we watched the longboat leave the beach heading back to our ship. The Captain was summoned from his cabin and he reached the deck as the longboat tied up beside us.

The sailor returning with the longboat stepped onto the deck asking to speak with the geologist. While she was being alerted, he described an orange glow he had seen emanating from beneath those clusters of stones between the bases of the towers and accompanied by an ominous trembling of the earth. The astronomer had confessed annoyance to the sailors who had accompanied her that these vibrations would reduce the precision of her observations. She then asked one of them to return to the ship and retrieve our geologist. The geologist, meanwhile, finally emerged from below just then and the sailor began to repeat his tale for her when someone called our attention to the island.

We watched two spots of light move rapidly, one ahead of the other, down from the rise and back toward the beach, except that their movements appeared frantic and confused. Flashing among the towers the lights of their lanterns burst into uncanny and baffling shafts of colors. Watching all of this our Captain ordered the sailor back into the longboat to return to the island and rescue the astronomer along with the second sailor and he sounded seriously concerned for their safety. Our anthropologist had stood among us listening to the sailor's report and now he insisted he join their rescue, but the Captain explained that he would not risk losing any more scientists.

The longboat with the lone returning sailor pushed off and we followed its progress. Meanwhile, the lights of the astronomer and the second sailor finally reached the beach but then followed the waterline first in one direction and then the other, all as if in a panic. Their movements were so erratic that the sailor in the longboat needed to alter its course in order to land near them.

Watching all of this from the ship left us frustrated, unable even to guess at what we witnessed. Our hydrologist then recalled that we had packed flares among our equipment and suggested that a lighted flare would help the longboat's sailor regain its path and perhaps also reveal whatever seemed to pursue our astronomer and the second sailor.

Fired from the deck the flare soared into the black sky hissing and trailing red and orange sparks arcing toward the island before it exploded with a piercing white light. Momentarily blinded, gradually we made out the sailor struggling in the longboat. With the beach now illuminated we saw our astronomer and the second sailor standing rigid as if startled. Yet beyond their figures which the flair's light outlined with hard black shadows we saw nothing. Under its tiny pale parachute the burning flair hissed and sputtered in slow descent and cast its pitch-black shadows around those glittering and sparkling towers while allowing us to follow the longboat until it beached. The sailor who had accompanied the astronomer climbed into the boat but somehow we lost sight of our astronomer as if she had taken a separate path and become swallowed by all of those conflicting shadows.

Our anthropologist had stood with us at the rail though at some distance away and his dismay was obvious. We now assumed our astronomer had seen the longboat and would join the sailors and return to our ship. But we had fallen into a false assurance that we understood what we were watching because suddenly and to our surprise our anthropologist removed his shoes and outer clothing, climbed to the top of the rail and dove into the black water. We called out for him to return but we were relieved that he seemed to be a strong swimmer. Although the beach was a distance away we convinced ourselves he would reach it safely, yet despite the light from the flair he disappeared from our sight. Several claimed they followed his progress and could just make out his wake, but at what moment he reached the beach, if he did so at all, none of us could be certain.

Finally we speculated that our colleagues were not alone on this island, if they ever had been. Whether they were in danger we could hardly surmise but we had to assume that was likely. And then the flare's light winked out as it dropped into the sea.

Despite the return of darkness we tried to follow the movements of the others on the beach. Perhaps it was an effect of our anxiety but considerable time seemed to pass before we realized the longboat was returning to our ship.

When it was close enough, we recognized that its additional passenger was the second sailor, but neither our astronomer nor our anthropologist was beside them. The Captain was furious that his sailors had returned without them and he ordered the second sailor who had accompanied the astronomer to recount everything he had witnessed.

The sailor looked about with the panic of a cornered animal and trembled as if gusts of chill wind crossed his skin. According to him, watching the astronomer make her observations had quickly left him bored so he began to wander. He noticed within a cluster of rocks nearby a glow that resembled the fading embers of a wood fire but which oddly seemed to brighten and dim accompanied by a weak sort of trembling beneath his feet. He then looked further to realize that this same glow appeared at other clusters and that these seemed to continue into the distance. When he brought this to the astronomer's attention she did not seem surprised and complained mildly that it was distorting her observations. She then asked him to return to the ship and bring the geologist. He had moved only a short distance toward the longboat when the tempo of those pulses of light increased and their lights became brighter. After a moment she suggested they both return to the beach and the longboat.

At first as they returned to the beach the astronomer followed the sailor looking about as if merely curious. He insisted he saw nothing as they returned to the beach that suggested they were in danger and he admitted surprise that she had seemed concerned. Then and for no reason he could see she sprinted past him suddenly, and despite the darkness and the uneven ground charged ahead, weaving frantically among those rock towers toward the beach. And then it was all the sailor could do to keep up.

Just as they reached the beach the light of the flare suddenly surrounded them. The sailor assumed that if there was danger nearby it would now be revealed. He called to the astronomer to stop, and to his surprise she did, but then she looked about as if fearful. By the light of the flair the sailor saw the longboat approaching and he called this out to her. He assumed then that she saw it as well, but instead of moving toward it, for some reason she turned and ran back up along the rise and toward the interior of the island. This confused him and he called out and then tried to follow her, but due to the shadows etched hard by the flair he could no longer make out a clear path and then she disappeared from his sight. Confused by what he should do next he remained on the beach hoping she would return. And then the longboat arrived.

We listened to his account astonished. The Captain ordered both sailors back into the longbow to retrieve the astronomer and the anthropologist. He then announced that we needed to abandon the island, at least until daylight returned.

We were all now ferocious with curiosity and frustration. While none of us could pretend friendship with the anthropologist, he had spontaneously and without regard for his own safety jumped into the sea determined to help our astronomer. We wanted to help her, but now we were obligated to help him as well. We watched the longboat make its slow progress back to the beach.

Upon their landing we watched the lanterns of the sailors move toward the interior of the island but had to guess at what we were seeing. Our geologist meanwhile expressed concern over the origin of that glow the sailor had reported and she speculated that active lava flowed dangerously close to the island's surface. She said that if that was the case, those on the island were in far greater danger than we had anticipated.

We repeated our appeal to the Captain to allow us to launch the second longboat and join the search. His timid hesitation left us frustrated. Our geologist insisted we be permitted our own attempt at rescue since members of our team were in a danger which he could neither understand nor measure and we were obliged to rescue them. After all, decisions concerning his sailors and his ship were separate from those which placed members of our team in danger, or that failed to resolve their danger. He remained reluctant until finally ignoring his protests and warnings we launched the second longboat and using those lights of the sailors on the island as our guide rowed for the island.

When we landed, our lanterns shone among those towers glittering and flashing in ways that startled and confused us. Following a path that kept us far from the towers and despite the darkness we began our search confident that after all, one could cross this island quickly even in darkness. But struggling to walk over its broken and uneven surface disguised by that darkness our progress was discouragingly slow.

Moving around the piles of broken stone forced us often to separate. But none of us could fail to notice those lights the sailor had described emanating from within mounds of rubble. Confused within all of that misdirecting light we called out to each other and in this way discovered that the towers distorted sound as much as they did light, and all of its reflections and distortions left us questioning what could be true.

But what also startled us were those subtle and frequent tremors beneath our feet that the sailor had reported. Despite our having spent an entire day exploring the island, none of us recalled having noticed them. Puzzled, our geologist conjectured that these vibrations might only occur after sunset. While this seemed absurd, she offered the further speculation that since our nightfall left the sun facing the side of the earth opposite to our island, the stress of the sun's gravity along with the force of the tides all combined with the island's unstable geology could leave the island sensitive to even very small stresses. Suddenly we recognized that if this was the case, we all were in far greater danger than we had even imagined. And then our geologist discovered that by moving closer to those piles of glowing rocks, the tremors beneath her feet became stronger. We agreed that we should avoid those clusters, but while doing this our chemist suddenly cried out. He had stumbled up to his knee into a shallow opening in the earth which none of us had noticed. He suffered no serious injury and we looked at the fissure more closely. The concern in our geologist's voice was unmistakable when she announced that we were now in serious danger.

A trill of panic passed through us and we looked about for a path that was safe. At that moment we recognized these delightful towers as ominous and threatening. And then, almost as confirmation, moving away from those towers our hydrologist stumbled into another fissure. But this was at a location we had walked across moments before, and we were certain its opening had not been there. Those subtle tremors continued as we watched this opening widen while it deepened. Utterly unprepared for this discovery we continued toward the beach hopeful that along the way we would encounter our colleagues.

Although we avoided that path which had brought us, as we moved we discovered more openings and some were wide and deep. Suddenly one of the glowing piles of rock exploded releasing a jet of steam with a hissing roar. Moments later another cluster of glowing rocks further off exploded. Determined to move away from these we discovered another fissure, but this one was sufficiently wide and deep to have swallowed any one of us completely. With this there was no longer any question; we would abandon the island to save ourselves and resume the search for our colleagues with the return of daylight.

We moved in the darkness attempting to avoid these openings along with the exploding vents, and as a result we returned to the beach far from our original route. But fortunately in this way our group managed to rejoin the two sailors. Even without the light of our lanterns we could see that they were pale with terror and relieved to see us. We learned that one of them had fallen into a particularly large fissure which had opened suddenly in their path and had only just been able to climb out with the help of the second sailor. They had not found either our astronomer or our anthropologist but they had reached the same conclusion we had; leave the island and wait for daylight.

With all of us except our astronomer and anthropologist reunited, and burdened with concern and regret we returned to the two longboats and made our way back to the ship. Relieved to have saved ourselves, from the longboats we watched the island still hopeful of recognizing a sign of our colleagues. And even after we reached the ship, several of us remained beside the rail and watched the island. Throughout the night we saw flashes of what we wanted to believe was the lantern of the astronomer but which we had to assume were simply more of those exploding vents.

That long and discouraging night was filled with distressing speculation which led nowhere. Finally the sun arose, but even before full daylight as many of us as could safely travel climbed into the longboats and returned to the island. Our plan was as simple as it was urgent; search until we found our astronomer and our anthropologist. Because the island was small, we landed confident that before sunset we would have peered into every location they could be lurking.

On the beach we divided the possible paths across the island among us and then set out. But we had not gone far when our geologist brought to our attention the absence of tremors. At first we suspected they were simply more subtle or less frequent, but soon we agreed they had stopped altogether and this seemed to support our geologist's conjecture. We tried to follow the path of the previous night and locate its fissures to confirm what we had seen. We hiked across the entire island, however, and failed to find a single opening. Suddenly those magnificent stone towers surrounding us were no longer beautiful. Despite their sparkling delight now glowing in morning sunshine their charm was gone. Our chemist wondered aloud why none of the accounts we reviewed had mentioned the exploding piles of rock or tremors or those fissures.

Of every question that could have been asked about the island, this one brought us all to a silent halt. We could only speculate that these phenomena had not been reported by earlier visitors simply because none had spent the night on the island. At that moment we looked about as if we found ourselves suddenly on an entirely new planet.

After several hours of walking we concluded that there were no openings or even marks of openings at those locations where we were confident they should have been. We turned to our geologist and once again she confessed she had no useful suggestion beyond what she had already offered, admitting that she was as baffled by all of this as the rest of us. Had the disturbances due to the motion of the planet resealed those openings shut, and even more dreadful, could any of those sealed openings now possibly enclose our colleagues? And then we asked ourselves whether, if we waited until evening, those fissures would reopen and allow us to rescue our colleagues, or at least recover their bodies? We discussed returning to the island after sunset for this purpose, but our geologist reminded us of the danger and then asked if there was any realistic way to conduct such a search. Our silence was our best, although least useful, response.

With our most urgent questions unanswered we resigned ourselves to recording our results and cataloging our samples along with all those questions our excursion had raised in the hope that those who followed us would return to the island better prepared than we. But our colleagues were lost and in a way by which they could not be recovered. Any revelations resulting from our research seemed trivial consolation for their loss.

ISLAND OF THE DISAPPEARING CAVERN

WE BEGAN OUR VOYAGE assigned by our institutions to gather evidence concerning an obscure legend that a piercing light once had arced across the sky leaving in its trail the aroma of orange blossoms and depositing a mass of land in the middle of the ocean. This account was common within the region but as a result of corrupted documents the particular island at its center proved difficult to identify. But recent though seemingly unrelated revelations had captured the world's attention and suddenly there was a fierce competition. We had been gathered at the last moment under confused circumstances and our individual areas of expertise were more valued than any demonstrated ability to collaborate. We were at sea for some time and this experience exposed ours as an uncomfortable and disharmonious team whose bickering sarcasm had become the inevitable response to even our most idle remarks.

And more, our expedition had been organized on such short notice that the only captain who's ship was available for our voyage had already committed his ship to a separate journey. Thus, we had to agree that once we landed he would continue to that second destination and so, for that time we would be without his support. Given all that followed, it is difficult to ignore the likelihood that the prospect of our isolation on the island stimulated an anxiety which could only be relieved through physical intimacy even while that anxiety amplified our pervasive irritability. Although worthy of analysis, our speculation now is that this disorienting sexual anxiety compelled those inappropriate decisions which fractured our team. There was as well perhaps a certain unanticipated hostility among us; as if beneath our façade of collegial politeness there was a void providing a reservoir and all of our professional jealousy could only be dissipated through sex. Further consideration need not detain us here, but the power of that terror of abandonment must not be ignored as a critical factor. Ironically, that same anxiety which threatened our enterprise eventually, though inadvertently, provided its success.

Assured by our Captain that he would return for us within six days of our landing, after a brief circuit of the island we loaded three longboats with our entire team along with our supplies. We landed and off-loaded on a portion of the beach near the opening to a valley which appeared to traverse the island splitting it neatly in half and with a small and glittering stream flowing through its center.

As senior members of the expedition, our geologist and our botanist supervised the establishment of our base camp. Thus, although unplanned, our expedition from its beginning labored under divided leadership, and in hindsight perhaps it was this division, a management issue after all, which provided the fertile soil for all that followed. It demanded most of that morning to establish our camp, and once completed we entered the valley to discover that something subtle and inscrutable immediately began to affect us. We did not remark this to each other at first, but we each experienced a delicious irritation like the preview of a sneeze along the surface of our skin that left us particularly sensitive to touch, which then and even more oddly manifest as a thrill of desire. Curious and excited without knowing quite why, we failed to guess this valley could contribute to our antagonism and by the time we did it was already too late.

Of course we were never honest with ourselves or each other about what we experienced or how this world suddenly appeared to us, and perhaps had we done so all that followed might have been avoided. Instead, we horded our perceptions and jealousies and resentments as if expecting to deploy them later and for some advantage.

Seduced by that stimulus from the valley, by the end of that first day we each already had drifted into self-obsessed conjectures that led us to imagine ourselves embattled, each against all in a universe of hostile forces. Upon reflection later, some insisted that as ambitious academics the pressure we endured to achieve results caused our camp to degenerate into a squalid nest of combative and hyper-sexual antagonists, as if success in such conflict might advance our careers. Bitter words and lascivious glances eventually accompanied each of our activities until, though we failed to recognize it, we were tested in ways for which we were inadequate. Thus, eventually only food and sex, demanding at least brief cooperation, brought us together although never completely nor for very long.

At our meeting after the evening meal our entomologist reported that despite the island's prodigious flora, to her surprise and confusion she had encountered no insects. The rest of us were so startled by this that it led to instant contradiction. Our geologist asked derisively how those flowers we had seen were fertilized without penetration by insects. His words were followed by guffaws and giggles and this should have assured us of that unacknowledged tension already overwhelming us. But at that moment we would only admit we were insulted at being asked to believe that insects, which must be present, hid from us. We retired to our tents burdened by a perverse distrust we refused to acknowledge though it left us as annoyed and depressed as teenagers.

Unwilling to leave the question to further research, the next morning our meteorologist, a member of the geologist's team, insisted that while this was not his area of expertise he was certain that as a result of either professional ineptitude, carnal distraction or simple indifference, our entomologist had botched her survey. Our chemist, also a member of the geologist's team, regretfully agreed and then named team members who had urged him the previous evening to consent to a panoply of sexual intimacies, all of which, he insisted, would interfere with his research. Response to this was embarrassed head-shaking accompanied by comments concerning professional conduct, but those individuals named offered no denials. We could not yet acknowledge our crippling problem or that distraction to which we were being driven.

Gathered for our second evening meal, the botanist's team confessed its suspicion that the flora of the island was impossibly unique and this suggested an explanation for the absence of insects. Because according to their research not a single plant or flower resembled any of those found beyond the ridges that surrounded our valley. And even more startling, no two plants growing within our valley appeared entirely alike. They suggested that due to the absence of insects along with those birds they would attract, each plant was a unique expression of its dominant form, a genetic formality that included all of its variants. Our geologist queried our botanist derisively over how, if these plants reproduced by parthenogenesis, they avoided being identical from generation to generation?

Our botanist appeared confused and insulted by the question but she was adamant about her conclusion. According to her baffling analysis, since each specimen represented only itself, any catalog of specimens would amount to nothing more than a disorganized list. Members of her team, meanwhile, displayed darkly-circled eyes so that the rest of us assumed exhausting bouts of intercourse had polluted their results and so their purported evidence must be ignored.

On the other hand, and perhaps as a result of some inherent sexual resilience, the geologist's team managed to perform a detailed survey of the island and concluded the geology of our valley resembled none of the rest of the island. According to this, our valley's geology was so aberrant and unlikely that it could have dropped from the sky complete and intact. They admitted that they failed to identify specific evidence of that impact other than the valley, but insisted the valley could not be the result of erosion or some uplift and resembled a fracture resulting from an impact. They then speculated that the impact had created a void or space beneath the valley which remained to be discovered. They conceded that the geological event they described verged on the impossible and so its proof demanded that we locate this void.

Our derision for their speculation was even more adamant than it had been for the absence of insects but it shocked the rest of us into a brief sobriety. As unlikely as it was, if their analysis was correct we had stumbled upon a unique object of investigation. Yet following this announcement, instead of pursuing their hypothesis with additional research, the geologist's team simply got the rest of us drunk. Loquacious in their inebriation, they described their strategy of research as sleeping locked together in passionate embraces, and worse, when not embracing within their tent, traveling together purportedly in search of this unlikely yet necessary void, but in fact going nowhere except crazy.

By the end of the third day our situation had become critical. Earlier, our geologist had gone with our botanist to carry our canteens to the stream to be refilled. Their accounts upon returning of what had happened at the stream differed. Our geologist claimed he merely slipped on wet rocks as he filled a canteen, while our botanist insisted the bruise on his forehead was evidence of her defense from his unwanted advance. As a result, the botanist's team stated it could no longer collaborate with the geologist's team. Our camp had become paralyzed by suspicion and mistrust.

Later that day, several of us met together informally, determined at least to summarize the progress of our research. The rest of us remained confined to our tents either conspiring over strategies for revenge or engaging in sex. But most engaged in sex.

Our situation could not continue and we understood this. But a whole day needed to pass before the inevitable occurred.

We awoke the following morning to the sound of the botanist's team packing their tent. They claimed they had found a better campsite and in word and tone made it clear they would not tolerate interference. Our meteorologist asked if our expedition was breaking up. Our botanist responded that on the contrary, we would make more progress if each team followed its own path of research.

Several of us instantly foresaw a tussle. When the entomologist of the biologist's team was grabbed by the mineralogist of the geologist's team, he insisted his team was one woman short. Our botanist then signaled her colleagues to take the chemist with the justification that she could never find enough cooperative men or sober chemists. The rest of us knew she was getting the worst of the bargain but we assumed she planned to keep the chemist from following the mineralogist. Perhaps she hoped his presence might even lure the mineralogist to their tent.

By mid-day intemperate words had been exchanged, the botanist's team had moved off and the geologist's team retreated to their tent to engage as they wished. Near twilight and as anticipated, our chemist attempted his escape, but without the mineralogist's help he became instantly lost and only accidentally found his way back to the botanist's camp.

But suddenly and for no apparent reason, those team members who had been sleeping together since our landing were no longer getting along, perhaps finally mistrustful of all alliances. Instead, the paleontologist spent the evening cleaning his revolver, while the botanist cut her negligee into bandages and then sharpened her machete.

At the geologist's camp, after a boisterous but inconclusive meeting, the meteorologist enumerated the remaining opportunities for research regretful that the teams could no longer successfully collaborate. Hearing this the geologist became furious, and the meeting ended in merely one more parody of intellectual distraction. Eventually, in stealth and shrouded in darkness, individuals escaped their camps eager to engage in pairings that involved members of antagonistic groups as opportunities for the exchange of research results among other things. As a result, in order to accumulate useful data, this arrangement compelled numerous collaborations.

And then the botanist and the biologist found the cave.

The geologist's team already had found numerous caves along the opposing ridges of the valley, but those had been small and shallow and of no particular significance. But this cave was different.

In a startling way, with its discovery all of our conflicting speculations seemed suddenly to converge and suggest our true situation. Even our botanist was compelled to agree the valley must be a split in the surface of some enormous mass embedded in the surface of the island and that the terrain beyond was composed of debris thrown up by its impact. Although our data, wrongly interpreted as it was, had demanded the existence of a void, this could only be a conjecture until the cave was found.

The particulars of their discovery need not detain us, except that in their search for greater privacy our botanist and our biologist had followed the valley to where its ridges converged into a narrow gully. The cave's entrance had been covered by overgrowth so densely entangled and thorn-ridden it had been missed by the geologist. In hindsight we wondered how, considering these circumstances, they could have made this discovery but we decided not to ask.

Fortunately, discovery of this cave brought our conflicting teams together. The cave was deep and its exploration would demand our combined expertise. For the moment, by inflating each personal ambition, the urgency of its discovery overwhelmed every other lust.

Still, some remained prepared to conflate our data and pollute its reliability if it proved personally advantageous. Thus, we were forced to recognize that any claim could already be false. Envy, jealousy and self-important ignorance was that morass which we claimed to despise, yet we swam in it as casually as a warm bath.

The cave's entrance was just wide enough to allow each of us to enter singly. Along its floor ran a small stream we realized fed into that stream whose water we had been drinking since our landing. Near the cave's entrance, that stream disappeared among loose rocks and only re-emerged far down the valley and so for this reason its path had failed to lead us to this cave. When our chemist analyzed its properties that fluid responded positively to every test, no matter how unlikely its result appeared, as if it included every element in the periodic table. Though confronted by one more paradox, none of us was yet prepared to trust the research of anyone else, so our agreement to explore this cave could only be a reluctant exercise in resentful cooperation.

Within steps of its opening the cave broadened as its path climbed. In that eternal darkness the lights from our lanterns dipped and zoomed like drunken fireflies over irregular ceiling, walls and floor. Further inside the path suddenly broadened into a large chamber with a wide shallow pool at its center, the apparent source of that stream flowing along the valley. To our surprise, the chamber was surrounded by openings to smaller caves, each a source of its own stream that fed the central pool. Despite our lanterns the ceiling seemed to disappear above our heads and our softest whisper echoed. There would be no secrets in this cave.

The chamber formed an imperfect circle and we walked around the pool scrutinizing the chamber walls and peering into the smaller cave entrances while our geologist took samples of the rock surrounding us. Though none of us spoke of it, we recognized that we would need to explore each of these caves if only to locate the source and nature of their inexplicable fluids. Our geologist called us to the entrance of one of these side caves and pointed out markings just beside it in the dark stone walls. These figures resembled either prisms or triangles or stars, but more disturbing, each implied something more than an accident of nature. With this our pit of speculation opened, all of us fell in and none found the bottom. Assumptions congealed, contention boiled, postures stiffened.

It remains uncertain whether it originated with our biologist or entomologist or even our botanist herself, but when it was speculated that considering the possible origin of the geology surrounding us, the creators of these figures might have arrived from beyond our planet, every voice became silent. Our chemist insisted there was no evidence for this but our botanist replied that given these circumstance it must be regarded as a justified conjecture.

Still, this was a possibility none of us wished to contemplate, and true to our self-image as conscientious researchers, we argued over even its plausibility. Those marks, however, resisted explanation without suggesting a strategy to either confirm or disprove any conjecture. Exploration of each cave to its end seemed to offer our only hope to resolve our questions.

As we began to plan our exploration we discovered that the number of caves and the number of paired team members was identical. As contentious as our relationships remained, it suggested an obvious research strategy.

Our geologist then reminded us there was no way to know which cave was safe to explore, if any, and so prudence dictated that pairs of team-members explore each cave. He admitted that this might prove complicated but it assured the greatest safety while allowing the most efficient use of our limited time and resources.

After an exchange of muttered antagonisms the botanist recommended that each team be comprised of a member of either group. It was then asked how we would learn if a team was in trouble, and we agreed to reassemble at the central cave within one hour so that any who failed to appear would be assumed in trouble and the rest of us would pursue their rescue.

Efficient as this plan appeared, we returned to the problem of how to organize each pair of explorers. Again we fell into mistrustful contention when the geologist suddenly grabbed the biologist's hand and they disappeared into a nearby cave.

This action, although impulsive and arbitrary, compelled the rest of us to pair-off and begin the exploration of the caves. With this, things became complicated.

As we began our explorations we discovered that, perhaps due to some vapor surrounding us, each of us assumed a different time so that each pair of explorers returned to the central cave at different intervals. What occurred during those intervals remained unspoken, but for all that we could judge, considerable time passed before our entire team reconvened.

But once re-gathered we agreed that although surprisingly deep, none of these caves offered any feature which made it exceptional. Floors and walls were smooth although irregular and our geologist conceded the stone around us was consistent with that of an asteroid. The path of each cave moved from side to side becoming neither broader nor more narrow, and each ended with a small tight turn which resembled the hook of a question mark. Oddly, the walls and floors were variously marked with faint horizontal incisions parallel to the floor which suggested that something had moved through each cave. These marks differed from cave to cave without offering a pattern. Finally, within that hook at the far end of each cave was found a bright and burbling spring which was the source of the stream that emptied into the central basin. Although those incisions seemed suggestive we avoided the question of sentient agency. And we refused to speculate that such sentience might not be from our planet. There are some questions for which all answers are bad.

We considered additional speculations which, no matter how they were combined, refused to harmonize into a demonstrable conclusion. Empty of fresh ideas, eventually we fell silent. While the rest of us struggled with what appeared inscrutable, our geologist turned his lantern up to play its light over the ceiling. This time, within its yellow cone of light appeared a yellow fog accompanied by a faint sound that resembled the crackle of a wood fire. As we watched, that fog thickened until it resembled a yellow cloud.

We held our breath in anticipation although nothing more appeared to happen. But then we noticed a fine dust begin to drift down. Suddenly our geologist turned and began to run back toward the cave entrance. More curious than alarmed, the rest of us ran to follow.

Blinded at the entrance to the cave by the sudden sunlight we saw our geologist continue to climb toward the top of the ridge and we scrambled in pursuit. When finally we joined him we noticed beneath our feet a subtle, undulating motion which gradually became more violent, and then our geologist called out for us to step further back. We had only just done this when, with a powerful and rumbling roar followed by an immense geyser of gray-brown dust, the ground before us collapsed. As the dust settled we moved to the edge of what was now an enormous circular hole we recognized as the cave's central chamber but was now filled with enough rubble to cover those openings to the smaller caves. But it demanded several more moments of astonished silence to realize that the bitter contention we had endured had just as suddenly disappeared.

We stood around that circular opening looking at each other as startled as if we had all just awoken from the same horrifying dream. We saw each other now as if for the first time while disturbing memories of the previous days came to each of us in waves of embarrassment. Sunlight beat down yet we took no notice, frozen instead by what poured through our minds as a movie to which we were reluctant witnesses and which left all of us silent and ashamed.

But then, with a series of sharp sounds resembling gunshots, large cracks appeared among the rubble at the bottom of the cave. And then for only a moment we glimpsed through those widening cracks a black void whose dimensions we could not even guess. Those fractures of the ground continued to spread until their fingers approached the edge beneath our feet. But by now our danger was obvious and we had begun to run down along the valley and back toward the beach. But those spreading fractures followed us nearly as quickly as we moved. We reached our longboats, clambered in and began to row as we watched those openings follow. Finally some distance out to sea, to our horror we watched one entire side of the valley with a grumbling roar collapse and disappear from our sight. With more thuds and crashes, fragments of the opposing side of the valley began to slip away beneath geysers of dust.

We rowed frantically, determined to put as much distance as we could from this bizarre event. Confused and terrified, we watched those fractures reach that portion of the beach where our longboats had laid. Portions of the island continued to crumble beneath more fractures that raced toward the beach. Suddenly, sea water now bright yellow with sand from the beach grew into a yellow wave which filled those fractures pouring into that expanding void which had consumed so much of the island. Moments later and to our shock, the remaining portion of the island collapsed to disappear into that void and was followed by a sea wave of water so great its movement dragged our three boats toward its opening.

Panic overwhelmed us and screaming at each other like terrified children we pulled at the oars yet our boats drifted rapidly to approach that void. And suddenly with a great wet sigh the rest of the island collapsed to disappear beneath the waves. In the next moment the sea calmed so that it appeared as if we had not watched what we had just seen, that surface suddenly as placid as a lagoon. Within moments our rowboats drifted to that location over the spot on the island where, just minutes before, we had stood.

And then we were alone in our three longboats adrift on a featureless sea and with our rescue ship still days away. When finally we were able to speak we looked at each other with such startled expressions we might have been dropped a moment before into this location from far away. We began to speculate over what we had just witnessed, but we did not speak of our concern over how we might survive until we were rescued by our now-distant Captain.

Our meteorologist, recalling the large cave, suggested we had explored a meteor itself somehow already nearly hollow, and due to geological stresses along with our sudden presence had collapsed falling into that void which its impact had created. But our geologist politely questioned this by asking what space that soil impacted by the falling meteor had collapsed into. The botanist suggested that space might have been the vacated cone of an extinct volcano, leading our volcanologist to smile reminding us that volcanoes leave no voids. But our biologist countered that simply because such had never been recorded did not mean it could not happen, and that for all we knew the cone of that volcano had been void very far down. The challenge to explain all that we had seen and experienced remained, and neither our volcanologist nor any other member of the team could offer an account that explained each of its elements.

Our zoologist then speculated that what we assumed had been a meteor in fact might have been a sort of extraterrestrial egg whose occupants had lived in those tunnels we had explored but which, at some moment before our arrival, had hatched and those creatures fled, leaving that shell we assumed was a meteor precariously vacant, and that now, for all we knew we could be surrounded by those extraterrestrial occupants lurking beneath the surface of our sea. With this speculation the rest of us were reduced to frightened silence.

We looked about us then and realized that whether or not those occupants surrounded us, it was as if that meteoric egg along with that island where it landed had never existed. And absent that island, our Captain nearly failed to find us, as if without our intriguing island we were not.

THE ISLAND OF THE LOST SAILOR

THIS ISLAND HAD NOT BEEN MARKED on our maps nor had its existence been noted in that history or any of those legends which we reviewed in preparation for the voyage which originally we had planned to another island that lay several days' journey further away. While we needed to assume this island had existed some moment before we saw it, for all of that it could have appeared during the darkest part of the previous night. So when we spied it on the horizon glinting in the morning sun, we were startled and worried that somehow during the night our ship had strayed far off-course. But once our Captain confirmed our coordinates, and despite the risk to our schedule, our team was instantly eager to explore its apparition. By succumbing to the desire to explore a previously uncharted island we risked a great deal more than we recognized, but we were weak and its temptation overwhelmed our common sense. So there is less to wonder about in our decision than might at first appear.

Such opportunities, of course, remain exceptional. We justified our decision by agreeing that we had stumbled upon a discovery potentially grand enough to eclipse even those observations we expected to make on the island of our original destination. And yet several of us resisted this detour, insisting we could discover nothing on this unexpected island whose importance could match those observations we had planned so carefully to make and over such a long period of time. But those most eager to explore this island insisted that the compelling argument was also the most obvious; we could not know what might be discovered until we went there and looked. This argument is difficult to contradict since it asserts the laudable principle that any knowledge is superior to every ignorance.

But should we exchange a carefully planned study for another that might result in the gathering of mere data? The risk of failure following either course was significant but differently calculated and with different outcomes. Suggestions were proposed and arguments offered, but in the end our conclusion was just as several of us silently had assumed from the moment that island had first been sighted.

From where we dropped anchor the island appeared a wide and shallow bowl. Surrounding the island and beginning just beyond the high-water mark of the beach, a steep and narrow ridge soared gray and brown and festooned with patches of green vegetation to an intimidating height. But nothing beyond that ridge was visible. By this we speculated that the terrain within fell away and did not rise again before reaching the other side of the island. We conjectured an entire world at the center of this island, and many of us found that expectation itself compelling. From it we wove fantasy with speculation recognizing that nothing would be either denied or confirmed until we went to the island and looked.

And that simple accumulation of conjectures finally compelled even those inclined to avoid this island to agree instead to make a landing. Their only condition was that, regardless of what was found, at an agreed upon time we would return to the ship and proceed to our original destination and conduct our research according to our original plan.

At our request the Captain sailed around the island while we watched from the ship's rail hopeful we would recognize a break in that formidable ridge which would provide us an entrance. But after several hours completing that circuit we found nothing.

We were determined to accomplish at least a general survey in the limited time we had given ourselves, so a crew of four from our team along with a member of the ship's crew was gathered and we launched the longboat. Some were concerned that although the island was not large, a treacherous climb to the top of that ridge would demand most of our limited time. So when our longboat struck the beach, we confronted the problem of getting beyond that ridge and quickly. From our ship its climb had appeared difficult yet manageable. But standing at its the base we found that it was nearly vertical, and although its sides were rough we recognized few obvious footholds, and so we were compelled to admit that its climb would be both difficult and dangerous.

Without obvious handholds in the rock or a hidden ravine providing passage through, we understood that none of us had sufficient skill or experience to accomplish the climb. Discouraged, we followed the beach for a time hopeful of finding an opening we had missed from the ship but still found nothing. We resisted surrender and return to the ship, but we could not see an alternative.

Then to our surprise the sailor who had guided our longboat offered to make the climb himself and trail a rope which the rest of us then could use to follow. His name was Enrico, and at first we thanked him for his offer but politely refused, reminding him that as a member of his Captain's crew he was not obligated to take such a risk. But Enrico's grin as he insisted the climb was easier than it appeared disarmed us. He claimed he neither feared nor risked injury. Reluctant but still without an alternative, finally we agreed and repeating our gratitude we urged him to take every precaution.

And we were relieved to see that he proved as accomplished at climbing as he had claimed. His ascent was slow but he appeared sure-footed and each of his steps was certain. From time to time, as a result of the uneven features of the ridge, he disappeared from our view but moments later reappeared signaling that he would continue to advance. He was even more skillful than we had expected and for this reason we became optimistic.

Watching his progress up that sheer cliff-face, we exchanged speculations of what we might find on the other side and what we would do if our discoveries proved to be significant. In this way we passed the time as our sailor continued his ascent. And perhaps it was in the midst of a particularly animated disagreement that he disappeared from our sight and we lost track of him.

One among us claimed to have watched Enrico reach the summit before he disappeared, but those who had not seen this remained skeptical. We had asked that when he completed his climb he signal to us, but if he had done so none of us had seen it. His rope appeared to be anchored to a peak at the top of the ridge and so we were compelled to assume he had at least reached the summit. We waited for him to reappear, but when he did not we called out his name. It was impossible, of course, for us to know if our voices were heard at that distance.

Eventually one of us tugged on that rope he had left trailing behind him and concluded it was secure. Immediately our geologist began to climb. Using that rope she reached the top of the ridge quickly and with surprising skill. Our concern for our missing sailor remained but we continued to assume he would soon reappear. Having reached the top she waved for the rest of us to follow.

Although the climb demanded some time for each of us to complete, when finally we gathered at the top we agreed that the effort had been rewarded. The view from the ridge toward the interior of the island startled us. Sparkling green foliage filled the bowel-like depression that formed the interior of this island, and it was so dense we could not identify a single physical feature below us. It seemed as if a dense green cloud filled the center of the island which would never dissipate.

Our climb confirmed our first speculation that the ridge formed the edge of a depression but we had discovered that it was covered by a forest so dense we could not see beneath it to the ground. Close to the center of this forest we noticed a glint that suggested the presence of a body of water larger than a pond. Our geologist then confirmed what appeared obvious to us; this ridge likely formed the edge of a volcanic crater whose entirety comprised this island. She speculated that, considering the amount of erosion of the ridge along with the density of the forest below, it was reasonable to assume this volcano was ancient and had been dormant for a long time. Thus disguised by its blanket of vegetation, the island appeared even more intriguing than we had suspected. We were eager to climb down into this jungle excited by the prospect of its exploration and what we might discover there. But to our confusion and concern, we failed to locate Enrico.

And more discouraging to our aspiration, we discovered that the walls of the ridge were even steeper and more featureless on that interior side than what we had just climbed. When finally we were all gathered at the top of the ridge, our geologist explained that while the rest of us had been climbing she had searched further along the ridge but had found no sign of Enrico. Her grim speculation was that at some moment he had lost his footing and his motionless body now lay below us shrouded within that tropical landscape.

In many places the ridge had eroded nearly flat but most of it was so rough it was nearly impossible to traverse easily on foot. But it was also barren of vegetation and so if Enrico had continued further there was no way we would have failed to see him. We decided to leave the rope anchored as it was and toss it down along the inside of the ridge where we could use it to descend to interior of the crater. But when we did so, we discovered that the rope did not reach its bottom and that somehow the floor within the crater was far deeper than outside. In this way we realized that even if Enrico had fallen into the inside of the crater and now needed our help, we could not provide him any assistance.

Confined to that narrow space at the top of the ridge we stood about confused by how we might proceed and what we might still accomplish. But then our geologist called our attention to an opening into the ridge close to where we stood. Tall and oddly narrow, it appeared to be the entrance into a sort of cave. Our first suspicion was that Enrico also had seen this opening and his curiosity led him to follow it, and with this our concern turned to optimism.

Lanterns in hand we crossed the threshold of the cave calling out Enrico's name. Hearing no response we looked for any sign he had entered ahead of us. A short distance within, the cave widened with a gradual downward slope. We called out again listening for his response but we heard only the wind singing through the heart of our cave. But, as our geologist reminded us, this passage of air assured us the cave was open somewhere further below, and might even reach the bottom of the ridge. But whether that opening would prove large enough to allow us to escape we could not know until we reached it

Puzzled by how this opening had come about, she then suggested that it was the remains of one of the volcano's vents, but despite this speculation she appeared as baffled by its existence as the rest of us. In an effort as much to explore the nature of the cave as to locate our sailor, she suggested we follow the cave down. Several of us confessed reluctance, preferring to return by the way they had arrived and then return to the ship and inform the Captain of his sailor's disappearance.

But others insisted that if we suspected Enrico had entered this cave, we were obligated to confirm this. After all, he had made the climb voluntarily and for our benefit, so we should be prepared to do the same. They suggested as well that upon returning to the ship without him, the Captain would assume that at least we had made some effort to find him no matter how feeble.

After some disagreement we were forced to recognize that admitting we had not tried to find his sailor would justifiably anger the Captain, and understandably he would refuse to lend us help in the future. So we agreed to follow the cave and search. As to what we would do if we did not find him we did not even speculate.

Further ahead the cave narrowed until it permitted us to move only in single file. The walls and floor of the cave were nearly smooth and our geologist suggested that a great deal of water had flowed through this passage and for a long period of time. Considering the location of the cave's entrance this was a complicated speculation to sustain but we could not doubt that time and erosion had altered it significantly. Unfortunately her speculation suggested nothing useful about the fate of our sailor. Moving forward with the aid of our lanterns we traveled only a short distance into the cave when we began to hear music.

Identifying that sound we heard as music is likely an exaggeration since we did not recognize it as music at first. It seemed that the weak breeze followed this passage moving past us, and within its narrow confines the dimensions and configuration of its passage provided the conditions for a resonance which gave the sound its unlikely musical quality. But we realized as well that the sound varied in volume and pitch in a way that seemed to resemble music. And that rise and fall in pitch suggested that somehow the shape and dimensions of our cave varied continuously. This, the changing shape of a stone shaft, seemed so unlikely we saw no reason to give it serious thought. But we could not ignore the fact that the further we moved into the cave the more pronounced that sound's musical quality became. The sound's tone did not rise or fall along a continuum, however, but changed at distinctly separate intervals like the individual keys of a piano, as opposed to the continuous slide of a trombone. And more, we marveled that by some unlikely configuration within the cave, what we heard did not possess a single tone but more resembled a chord with several pitches sounding simultaneously. These pitches offered odd harmonies sounding in unlikely sequences as if fragments of music had been thrown randomly together. We followed the cave's descent until suddenly it widened and its floor briefly leveled and here we were able to gather and confer. In the glow of our lanterns and surrounded by those sounds we sat down together to catch our breath but also to speculate.

Having stopped moving we discovered that the music also stopped changing and we offered conjectures about what all this might amount to. Some of us insisted they detected a pattern in the sound, and after all, music is simply a series of tones in a particular pattern. They suggested that variations in that pattern could only be intentional and could only be the result of decisions of an active consciousness. They admitted that this seemed absurd. Others insisted those variations of the tone suggested only that our cave, behaving as a column of air within a wind instrument, was varied by our presence. Conflicting conjectures resulted in vigorous disagreement. A compromise was suggested; our presence as we moved within the cave modified its column of air and for this reason it was not necessary for the cave itself to change shape nor was any consciousness beyond our own needed to be involved. But in response it was pointed out that the tones in the sound seemed distinct and their pattern of change was not continuous but leaped in wide intervals so that the continuing column of air hypothesis was insufficient. In hindsight it seems absurd that a group of material scientists could hold strong opinions about the source and nature of a fragment of sound or would insist it was some form of music. Confined within our stone chamber and surrounded by odd sounds and unlikely resonances, we marveled at its charm and the thrill it provided to us regardless of its source. After further deliberation we were compelled finally to agree that only natural processes surrounded us and so this sound could only be the result of natural, albeit random, processes. Whatever we found pleasing or intriguing required nothing beyond geology and physics.

To all of our surprise our geologist put forward an oddly nuanced suggestion and one that was also more difficult to dismiss. Assuming the non-human source of the sound, she reminded us that the primary operation of consciousness was the recognition and decipherment of patterns among the phenomena of the material world, and that all of this was accomplished without reference to intentionality. In short, she insisted that the operation of the human mind was to create apparent coherence. The weakness of this suggestion of course, was that if consciousness was capable of inventing patterns, how might those be distinguished from recognized patterns. Our discussion took on startling vehemence and our voices gradually became so loud and harsh it was difficult to image that Enrico, had he still remained within the cave, could have failed to hear us. Flowing back and forth between incommensurable convictions, our disagreement only broke off when our geologist reminded us that time was passing and we needed to reach the end of the cave and locate Enrico.

We advanced only a few steps when suddenly we were startled to discover the path within the cave dip steeply downward, and attempting to follow it our footing became treacherous. Oddly, at this same moment the sound that had surrounded us grew louder while somehow it modulated as if seeming to move and pass beyond us as a Doppler effect. Once again it was suggested that by advancing into this broader and deeper corridor our movements had modified the interior of the cave in such a way that changed the flow of air and so this was simply another example of our presence shaping sound.

Still further along, the cave's floor became level before suddenly forming a series of abrupt rises and sudden dips. Some of these were so extreme and followed each other so quickly we were often confused by the cave's changes of apparent direction until we found ourselves baffled and disoriented. While we knew we remained within that steeply intimidating ridge, the cave's enclosure had become an intolerable confinement within which we lost all directional orientation. At this moment we recognized that the end of this cave might just as likely open within the crater as onto the sand of the beach.

At the next widening within the cave we stopped and again attempted to gather ourselves. But by now several of us had lost patience with our adventure and insisted we move quickly to the cave's end. They demanded the opportunity to lead so they could move ahead as quickly as the cave permitted. Before the rest of us could agree they forced their way to the front. The rest of us followed as quickly as we were able, simultaneously confused and furious.

Further ahead the channel of the cave dropped so steeply it was difficult to maintain our footing and we struggled to keep from tumbling forward into each other. Beyond this the cave then turned suddenly before it became more level. Our geologist speculated that the path of the channel had encountered a particularly hard material and had followed a seam of softer stone as the line of least resistance but which caused the passage to become more narrow. In a darkness made more confusing by the broken beams of our lanterns we bumped against walls and jostled each other in what suddenly became, despite our determination to resist, a stumbling panic to reach the cave's exit. That desperation exposed something about ourselves which in our attempt to ignore our dread of this cave had remained disguised even despite our concern for Enrico.

But then and just that suddenly, we arrived. The cave brightened around us and in the next moment we stood together on the soft and shifting sand of the beach under full and hot sunshine. We had reached this opening so suddenly that we stood together blinded and squinting at each other in startled and embarrassed silence. The prow of our beached longboat stood close by, our ship sat perched upon the sea further out. So it demanded a few moments for us to realize that we had followed the entire length of the cave without finding any side-chambers or alternative paths and yet had failed to identify any sign of Enrico.

We considered what we might do next when one of us turned to see some distance away that rope we had used to climb the ridge, except now it lay splayed and coiled on the pale yellow sand. And to our astonished confusion the noose that had been secured to a peak of the ridge remained intact. We looked back up to the ridge hopeful we would see Enrico but we saw no one. Our geologist insisted she had checked that the rope was secure before we entered the cave and was confident it could not have slipped off accidentally. This discovery turned our thoughts into knots and jumbles which refused to untangle. We could no longer look at each other without embarrassed anguish. We discussed again attempting to circle the island in the hope there was a break in the ridge which we had somehow missed and would still allow us to pass. But it demanded less than a moment to acknowledge that we had little time left to extend our search and certainly not enough to complete such a journey.

Our geologist then urged that we return to the cave and follow it back upward, suspecting that somehow we had missed a turn or failed to notice a well-disguised passage. We reminded her that we had seen nothing like that in our descent but she insisted that only this explanation made any sense. Further, she suggested that such a passage might open on the other side of the ridge and Enrico could have followed it to emerge within the crater's jungle. Only this, she claimed, would explain how we could have missed him. Others contradicted, insisting that if Enrico was still alive he would already have signaled us. But in the end the rest of us agreed it was better to return to the ship and report to the Captain what had happened as well as what we had done, confident he would devise a plan that would resolve this issue.

Once again, disagreement was met with impatience. Some argued that our climb of that treacherous ridge had been justified by our dedication to research and that by abandoning our search we conceded our choice had been wrong. Others put forward the recognition that Enrico had risked his life and may even have lost it on behalf of our research, and because of this we were obliged to search until we found him. We were loath to reenter the cave, but with no other strategy available to us we agreed to follow our geologist.

Inside the cave we immediately encountered a rise in its path none of us recalled and which forced us to climb, and this proved difficult. Its smooth stone floor had been arduous to negotiate following it down from the ridge, but our attempt to climb by this same path proved impossible. Gravity, which had aided us, now only compounded our difficulty. To our frightened consternation, we agreed that our memories of the cave were that the course of the cave had been nearly flat but what we now found did not resemble the path we had followed.

Attempting to recall our path, we each described different recollections of its direction, but we agreed that this path resembled none of them. Within its narrow darkness our geologist insisted this new although treacherous climb still could be made, but when challenged she conceded that she was uncertain how best to proceed. Finally we agreed that, having failed to find Enrico, we should now report to our Captain what had happened and what we had done.

Even before our longboat reached the ship, sailors called out from the deck concerning Enrico. Despite a blistering sun, our reception once we stepped onto the deck was chilly. As we had agreed in the longboat, our geologist described for the Captain all that had taken place and all that we had done.

As the details of our tale were recounted, the Captain's face hardened, and when our report was concluded all eyes fell on him. Although he was neither a tall nor a broad man, his body seemed to enlarge with silent rage and the glare of his eyes became too fierce to meet. At the end of our recitation he reminded us with a bitter growl that he had agreed to deliver our team safely to our original destination and that this would be done. But he startled us when he turned to the first-mate informing him that he was returning to the island to rescue Enrico. He then ordered tents and firearms loaded into the longboat in preparation for an extended stay, and four sailors were chosen to accompany him. Having given these orders he then turned to our geologist to explain that the first-mate would take command of our ship and deliver us to our original destination. To the first-mate he then added that upon dropping anchor in port and delivering us to that island he should re-supply the ship as quickly as possible and then set sail to rejoin him.

The longboat loaded with supplies and piloted by the Captain and his crew set off for the island in time for our ship to catch the out-going tide, and then we watched the island sink below the horizon as our ship moved on. Although during our voyage to our original destination the crew cursed us regularly and singled several of us out for particularly vile threats, the rest of our voyage was uneventful and we arrived at our destination as scheduled. And just as expected, our ship under command of the first-mate set sail with the tide the following morning to return to that island.

As we had agreed for our previously planned research project we journeyed far inland and remained there isolated and unable to communicate with anyone in the port for several weeks, and for this reason we did not learn until we returned to the island's port that our ship had gone missing. Recognizing the ship's disappearance, a small flotilla had been sent out in an effort to find it or locate survivors. But the ocean is vast and no one beside our Captain and his first-mate knew the island's coordinates. In desperation we were asked by the port's officials if we could recall those coordinates, but unfortunately none of us had had the presence of mind to record them.

In this way the found is sometimes lost.

ISLAND OF GOLDEN EYES

JUST BEFORE SUNRISE we began to smell the island, and long before we saw it; an aroma pungent and sweet and pleasantly irritating. We had organized this voyage to investigate a legend according to which the origin of this island reached back to the earliest moments of our planet's existence, and beneath its surface lurked an enormous creature whose birth pre-dated that of the solar system. The variants of the legend agreed that the creature is of enormous size and came to rest on our planet as a stage in its gestation. Adrift within our accumulating solar system, it had become caught-up within that cosmic debris gradually coalescing to form our planet. This debris eventually surrounded the creature creating a shell. But most intriguing, according to this legend, as our planet's end approaches, this creature will break out of this shell to rise up and flee. Additionally, the legend claims that a slim vent resembling that of a volcano is attached to its shell allowing the creature to remain in contact with the universe and this opening should permit us to view the creature. Of course we were dubious of all of this, and yet the consistency among the variants of the legend proved compelling and demanded our investigation.

What we saw on the horizon at first was merely a pale cloud perched atop a brown smudge. Approaching closer, we recognized within that cloud and sheathed in glittering white the peak of a volcano-like feature and its appearance confirmed at least one element of the legend. But it was only near daybreak the following day that the island itself came into view, though our distance continued to disguise its ghastly nature and its threat.

Sailing closer, that aroma we had found so charming finally enveloped our ship as a bitter and miasmic cloud irritating our eyes and lips, and within which no birds approached while the sea presented a gelatinous surface iridescent and flat. Thus we confronted the island's deepest paradox; its conflation of sensation with thought, clarity with confusion, of enticement with danger.

Over several hours we sailed the circumference of the island until we found between outcroppings of coral a navigable approach. That search provided an overview of the island and from the deck of our ship our geologist identified a path he was eager to follow. Our doctor's tests of the atmosphere and water confirmed the presence of various subtly corrosive substances, and this suggested there was little possibility of life on the island. As our ship dropped anchor a delightful aroma resembling orange blossoms suddenly suffused the air, but our doctor's warning left us wary. Elements of the legend suggested the island's capacity to dissemble and disguise, so every pleasant sensation should have confirmed the depth of its corruption and its power to assault.

We invited our Captain, a tall, hard-built and thoroughly reliable man, to join our team and assume responsible for its safety. The rest of our team was comprised of our geologist acting as our survey's leader, our biologist who acted as our photographer, our chemist, our meteorologist, our mineralogist and our medical doctor.

From our ship the island appeared to rise gradually beyond the beach before becoming level until the volcanic vent near the island's center added its tower. Surrounding its base a fog of tints ranging from powder blue through rose swirled reaching smoky tendril-like fingers toward the peak of the vent before dissipating into a greenish sky. But we were startled to see spouts of geysers resembling those of whales which had not been mentioned in any version of the legend and this struck us immediately as curious. But as well-informed about the island as we believed we were, we failed to anticipate how thoroughly disorienting these features would prove to be.

Although from the ship we had first seen these geysers and heard their blasts, we needed to step onto the beach before we recognized that each erupted confined within its own burbling and frothy pastel pool. Transfixed by the profound grace of these geysers we were stunned by their deafening eruptions. We stood together beside the longboat intrigued by their colorful charm and still not yet frightened by their power. The dense atmosphere surrounding us filtered the sunlight casting both the sand and the water with a greenish hue. Our geologist speculated that those geysers were likely the source of the astringent gases and their aromas. The rest of us assumed this was likely true and yet we did not draw those logical conclusions which would have saved us from that confused bitterness which followed.

We made our way between those grumbling geysers as the greenish hue of the light shaded in places to dull orange accompanied by the aroma of freshly-cut mint. Led by our geologist we followed the most gradual path upward. On either side of our path the plumes of these geysers arose and spread and often we were forced to pause until they subsided in order to pass. Low mounds crusted with pale mineral deposits separated their gasping pools of hot, brownish mud and the fragile crusts of these mounds cracked wherever we stepped. Without vegetation to study, our biologist took photos while our geologist collected samples. But our progress was so slow that by the time the sun approached the horizon and a hot damp breeze flavored with the aroma of ginger and sage drifted around us we still had not reached the summit of the first ridge.

Observing from the rail of our ship, our geologist had suggested we investigate a peculiar outcrop whose appearance seemed significant. But upon landing we discovered that its path led through a bowl-shaped depression we had not recognized. Our doctor reminded us that chemicals in the atmosphere would likely concentrate there, and added that with even brief exposure, breathing those chemicals could cause injury. He then advised us to spend no more than twelve hours on the island. Our geologist protested that even a cursory survey would demand more time and he was reluctant to lose this opportunity.

Ominous and perverse in their dolorous regularity, these geysers towered as sentinels dominating a glittering and barren landscape and their miasmal atmosphere caused the ground between those pools to appear the color of wet slate. Pale steam and orange-gray foam roiling within each hot spring drifted as a ground-hugging fog which disguised lacy white fringes of crystalline mineral deposits. Although we trod carefully, those deposits shifted treacherously beneath our feet challenging our balance as well as our patience.

With twilight advancing and so little accomplished we agreed to remain on the island overnight. Our doctor repeated his protest but could not deny that the time needed to return to the ship complicated our efforts. Our decision left us with the task of finding a campsite safely beyond the geysers and their vapors. Lacking wood for a campfire and with every source of water both hot and poisonous with dissolved chemicals, we relied on those limited supplies we carried. Our doctor speculated that the brew of aromas surrounding us masked something he could not identify but which left him concerned. By the time we found a suitable campsite there was only enough daylight to erect our tents and prepare a cold meal. In place of a campfire we clustered our lanterns at the center of our group of tents. Whatever the secrets to this island, it seemed determined to keep them hidden.

Camped far from the crashing surf, our night was punctuated by the hiss and blast of those geysers invisible in the darkness, exploding on irregular cycles and releasing their baffling mosaic of aromas. One among us joked that our island resembled a huge calliope playing an eternally new musical score. Serenaded by this relentless cacophony and despite our exhaustion we remained awake late into the night. Eventually we agreed the island was antagonistic to our presence, yet its explosive melodies suggested an inexplicable empathy with human sensations, as if experiencing somehow what it was that we experienced. Its behavior suggested the island was aware of our presence but what this might mean if it was true we had yet to consider fully. And then sunrise provided the answer to that question, because during the night we each experienced a disturbing disorientation.

The legend had suggested we should anticipate this as part of the island's self-defense, and so we had been warned of its antagonism. Although we had assumed it was mere metaphor, the legend described how, when the island became aware of alien presences, spontaneously it exhaled debilitating vapors to discourage invasion. While we were confident this was unlikely, we found ourselves compelled to acknowledge these distortions with embarrassed good humor even while their effects seemed too complex to describe.

Whether it was the effect of the chemicals in the air or the cacophony of explosions or the resulting sleep-deprivation or some perplexing combination, each of us endured an oddly different vertigo which resulted in a perplexing misrecognition of the island surrounding us and even more problematically each other. Gathered together for a brief morning meal we each attempted to describe our confusions, and by this realized we were confused even about our confusions. To our doctor's relief however, we exhibited no symptoms of physical injury.

But disorientation threw each of us into a surly and vaguely hostile resignation so that conflict became inevitable. And worse, eager to believe there was one among us who could be relied upon, we ignored the likelihood of our doctor's confusion. Yet despite our bafflement we attempted to plan a course for our survey. Unfortunately, this led to such contention that we were forced to consider ending the survey and retreating to the ship. As the path of the green-tinted sun passed mid-day, the odor of rotten strawberries suddenly surrounded us. Though we attempted to continue our exploration, overwhelmed finally by our own confused sensations we invited our Captain to offer a suggestion.

Although he seemed reluctant, he reviewed those dangers we had encountered and then speculated about dangers we should anticipate as we advanced toward the volcano's peak and with this finally he urged us to return to the ship. Of course we ignored the likelihood of his confusion, as though it was possible that somehow he was immune. Despite the reasonableness of his suggestion we concluded that our best option was to complete our survey quickly. We failed to anticipate that each of us would soon regard the other with mistrust and then fear. Like some psychic corrosive, this confusion which bred our mistrust now twined among us as the tendrils of an acidic fog. With good-natured sarcasm we wondered aloud whether we could become so disoriented that confusion would reveal reality.

Ignoring our Captain's counsel we packed our camp and resumed our climb. In a counter-intuitive discovery, the higher we climbed the more numerous the geysers became and their explosions seemed more powerful than those nearer the beach. Our geologist speculated that the magma chamber of the volcano, if there was one, became closer as we climbed toward its peak. Admitting his surprise he noted that this confirmed that our danger was greater than we had surmised. Our biologist then asked what the rest of us already wondered; was this new fact merely one more confusion, or was it a clue to the presence of something ominous beneath the surface? Our geologist suggested there were several plausible explanations while the rest of us found this one less than compelling. Our doctor then repeated that on this unlikely island it was possible the higher we climbed the greater our danger before he urged us to return to the ship. Grateful for his concern we were now even more determined to complete our survey.

As our doctor had warned, our confusion became more severe the further we climbed until we were forced to admit that our perceptions must no longer be trusted. With this we were compelled to recognize the true nature of our dilemma: how to conduct a survey when observations varied from researcher to researcher and otherwise could not be verified with evidence. We did not yet admit that the island was determined to disguise itself from us because we had refused to acknowledge that this island possessed intentionality.

As we climbed, the material environment gradually lost its materiality until our observations degenerated into mere conjecture and assumption. Visual distortions left us wandering in a dimensionless terrain of failed and shadowy recognition. We remained certain this island existed, but we could say nothing about it which we could demonstrate was true. Yet despite this, our determination to continue remained and foolishly we forged ahead.

Eventually and after the passage of an indeterminate amount of time with our Captain leading us we approached what we assumed was the vent's summit. Our doctor warned us that our danger had grown deeper with each step but our confusion reminded us that even he was no longer reliable. Advancing with the vile smell of some blend of noxious gases we could no longer identify surrounding us as we climbed, our Captain halted our progress often. Increasingly dense waves of illusion crashed against our reason leaving us depressed that our survey could no longer provide any certain knowledge. We approached absolute confusion leaving us as gleefully irresponsible as teenagers, though we assured each other that somehow we would soon resolve the island's mystery.

Enwrapped within layers of shapeless bewilderment the depth of our shared debility convinced our Captain we had drifted beyond recovery and that as quickly as possible we must return to the ship. But suddenly our doctor and our geologist refused to retreat, each warning that no one should attempt to stop him. For two men who had collaborated successfully for years this was out of character. When they walked away to continue their climb, the rest of us enjoyed something that resembled relief. But after a silent pause and despite our bewildered annoyance we followed as best we could.

Approaching the volcano's summit the aroma of over-ripe bananas billowed suddenly around us while the further we climbed the more exaggerated the terrain appeared with peaks like multicolored cones and sharply v-shaped valleys. Whether these combined effects were related we failed to conjecture. Even when two of us scrutinized the same feature, we each reported incommensurable results. The rocks as well as the composition of the sand and gravel along our path appeared to sparkle like bits of broken glass, but whether a material reality lay behind this observation we could only speculate. From our path what appeared glowing pink-orange light cast green and purple shadows scintillating like negative halos around those boulders resembling beach-balls which had begun to block our path as we climbed. Flat edges of pale crystals protruding from the edges of the hot springs sparkled with a light so fierce its illusion pierced our eyes.

Climbing further, the sky turned slowly to the color of pea-soup so that the declining sun appeared violet. Beneath our feet, the lattice-work of streams that seemed to cover the ground flowed as slowly as syrup as if laden with minerals, and they moved below a surface composed of that mineral crust left by evaporation along their serpentine journeys. The streams converged randomly, sometimes forming small pools before they disappeared. Under that uneven, green-tinted light and with the aroma of burnt walnuts now surrounding us their lacework appeared to float just above the ground so that when our feet sank through their thin crusts they disappeared within puddles of light.

Wheezing and coughing, finally we reached the last ridge. Cast by that uncanny light our shadows roiled over the ground like the wake of a boat across a windy pond. Fragments of re-formed crystals shifted erratically beneath our feet. The approach to the peak of the volcano appeared as a deceptively smooth upward slope and we were deluded into a confidence we would conclude our survey quickly.

Approaching the summit of the vent we were met by even more powerful vapors swirling from within its cone and flowing around us as a dense and bitter soup, and yet at its summit the view available to us left us startled. Our island appeared below us as a shattered kaleidoscope whose sparkling fragments alternately brightened and dimmed as a profound cascade of scintillating contrasts. Each of our distortions layered over the next suggesting clarity, yet this island refused our decipherment so that every perception of it was countered by a contradictory perception.

Our irresistible compulsion to act led finally to an argument which split our team into one group determined to return to the ship, and the other insisting we complete our survey. Despite his own confusion our Captain struggled as if determined to appear neutral. And we failed to realize that surrounded by these corrosive forces we had waited too long. Although we did not see this, our gravest danger now was that each of us would go our own way and this attempted survey would achieve nothing except our deaths.

None of us was prepared to concede it was possible the other had the better idea so argument, albeit without logic, point or purpose though still noisy and even hostile, continued as twilight threatened. But eventually we were forced to agree at least that our predicament had become dangerous.

No longer able to gather reliable observations, our convictions became our mental life-rafts suspending us above that bottomless tumult which was our ignorance and yet without enabling us to challenge that which appeared. We knew that we did not know what we assumed, but since our knowledge was no longer based on the evidence of our senses, we had no way to affirm our mistaken knowledge let alone recognize what might be true. Observation, that final assurance of certainty, had failed us and no amount of reflection could return it to us.

Those loud sighs of the volcano which we assumed we observed demanded that something was active beneath, but burdened by our multiple confusions, its nature could never be recognized by us no matter how many observations we attempted to collect. Nothing that appeared to impact our senses allowed us to distinguish between any illusions. Certainty dissipated into another aroma among aromas, another color blended from colors. Until we left this island, even the certainty of our uncertainty disappeared within the swirl of the apparently arbitrary and chaotic.

Yet we could not abandon what we remained convinced was an island until we reached what we assumed was the peak of its vent. We were certain we endured myriad assaults although we were unable to scrutinize them individually. As well, we failed to confirm even the existence of this vent although we remained convinced it was the main source of these confounding vapors. We resumed our climb optimistic that sufficient light remained to allow us to reach the top, and then it did.

Without recalling each step precisely, we found ourselves suddenly standing at the edge of that opening looking down as streams of vapors swirled around us, sometimes so dense that for long moments we could no longer see each other. In those moments we each experienced a startling sense of isolation, certain each of us now stood alone at the edge of a volcanic vent on an island in the middle of its own sea. Somehow we stood alone together, convinced that our simultaneity of sensation assured nothing which could resemble common experience. Even our Captain could neither confirm nor contradict any assertion made by any of us.

Looking down into what appeared to be the heart of this vent, each of us concluded we saw what we convinced ourselves must be enormous red-orange eyes and very many of them, blinking and brightening, rolling and staring as if aware and observing, perhaps even judging, as they returned our gaze. Even our Captain was tempted to assume he confronted a consciousness. We attempted to turn to each other for confirmation, yet awareness of these tremulous distortions left us unable to trust any perception. The corrosion of this mistrust blinded us until we failed to distinguish each from every other.

But were they eyes? Those which appeared to be eyes were numerous and enormous and fierce, colored a blend of old copper and tarnished gold, but above all suggesting an awareness within them which scrutinized our scrutiny. Or might they be instead pools and pockets of hot magma bubbling and churning, blooms super-heated and bright red-orange beneath dark and cooled crust in an eternally repeating cycle? Assuming these were eyes but too numerous to count and of such different sizes, all seeming to wink open and then shut while scrutinizing that which was infinity itself, but as a sequence of single instants, sparkling and shimmering as if only the fiercest fire could be the source of that light within their light. A conscious scrutiny, a scrupulous evaluation compelled us to identify that sign, that moment, the final stroke of the final hour of the final midnight.

Deep-throated vibrations from beneath our feet traveled through our bodies to reach our ears deadening our senses and fracturing our concentration. Perhaps this was the communication frequency of the creature's thought, a species of sympathetic resonance resembling an infinite harmonic amplifying within us each sensation which appeared to originate outside our senses. Could what we assumed were eyes in fact be accomplishing some other, although inscrutable, purpose? Perhaps we saw eyes merely because we needed them to be eyes and of a beast whose existence we had struggled to confirm. If they were eyes, could their consciousness recognize our curiosity or our fear? Even more, might those eyes be listening to our thoughts? And most confusing of all, could those eyes be speaking to us, addressing our minds while our ears remained deafened by the rumble beneath the vent and those blasts of the geysers? In fact, could what appeared to us to be eyes combine all of the beast's senses and thereby provide it a complete range of our sensations and all of this through their detection of resonant frequencies? If this was the case, these frequencies must have been specific to each of us individually; just as this creature might transmit and receive such signals, we each remained tuned to a specific and limited frequency even while the distinction among those frequencies assured our individuation.

Peering down together simultaneously but individually, at that moment we recognized that in the end such individuation had been the primary objective of our journey. Perhaps it was merely another unanticipated effect of these distortions, but as we stared down suddenly we recognized that individuation itself was at the center of every activity we had engaged in and everything we had attempted to discover. By our efforts to reveal and disclose a material reality surrounding us we each had hoped to assure our individual existence even if, without an appeal to evidence, this could otherwise never be proved.

Having succeeded in our ultimate failure, when that multitude of enormous eyes at the heart of that towering vent stared back at us as if acknowledging our unique existences we were free, released finally to descend and return and resume.

In this way and for this reason we came away from that vent and those eyes with the sensation of having seen something which had seen us, and with the sensation as well that our baffled consciousness had impinged on the consciousness of a being so profound that it transcended every history. A creature whose harmony with the universe generated waves of a subtle but pervasive energy at frequencies which had energized our awareness, permitting us to affirm even while we remained uncertain of that which we were aware.

Our Captain had been as incapable as the rest of us to discern these subtle and conflicting energies and yet he had remained confident of this material world which continued to demand our navigation and negotiation. Having assisted us in reaching our goal, he moved on within that world without leading us, like a boat traveling across water whose wake we were invited to follow. His movements, although imprecise and indistinct across a terrain which remained for us uncertain, enabled us to progress in retreat unconcerned and without reflection until we found ourselves again aboard our ship.

But was that creature, if what we believed we had seen was the creature, preparing to flee? Had it attempted to communicate to us one last warning but, unable to decipher its message or its intention, had we failed to recognize the bit of information that had been offered to us? Was the end beginning? We could only wonder without the assurance of material evidence.

ISLAND OF SLEEPLESS GHOSTS

THE INFORMATION AVAILABLE concerning those ghosts inhabiting the island was fragmentary but we were assured by every report that once we landed we would certainly encounter them.

Our team had been assembled with the intention of documenting these ghosts and we were well-educated, well-trained and thoroughly experienced in every relevant area. So we were confident that incontrovertible knowledge would result from our efforts.

Unfortunately we were also pedestrian thinkers, and for this reason our first assumption was that we would be unable to observe these ghosts before nightfall. This was corrected the moment we landed on the beach.

We crossed the breakers under a bright sun and with a mild breeze and beached our longboat before we noticed the sandcastles. Of course we were startled. Their tallest structures were knee-high and each layout appeared about the size of a card-table, but we needed to stand directly over them to recognize their level of detail. Of those thirteen castles we scrutinized, all followed the same general layout while each included distinctive variations so that no two were exactly alike. Strolling further along the beach, it appeared that its entire expanse of golden sand was dotted with these constructions and they continued for as far as we could see. With so much bright sand still unexplored, we had to concede that these could only be ambitious ghosts. We had not yet pondered the question of intention nor how we might understand these constructions.

We had journeyed to this island on the assumption there could be only a finite number of ghosts, another exercise in pedestrian thinking. With certain regularities among these sandcastles and with peculiar choices from one layout to the next, we were tempted to speculate a limited number of minds were at work and we were inclined to attribute personalities to their creators. Simply as imaginative creations, by their choices these ghosts had exposed enough of their intentions to allow us to draw defensible conjectures about their creators. We had not yet begun to speculate over where these ghosts had come from and why they remained confined to this island, and none of our documents had suggested answers. But uncovering answers to those questions as well as others justified the size of our team and our variety of skills.

These structures convinced us that their creators now stood invisible around us scrutinizing us as we scrutinized their creations. But despite several ingenious conjectures we recognized nothing in these structures that suggested any intention. We speculated that perhaps toward the center of the island the ghosts felt less exposed and so would be more likely to provide decipherable indicators.

From our ship the vegetation on the island had appeared sparse though concentrated in dense stands separated by wide areas of bright sand. Moving up from the beach under that full sunshine we were uncertain what the evidence for the origin of these ghosts might look like or how we might recognize it, but we assured each other that we needed simply to remain alert and we would know that evidence when we saw it.

The island's terrain rose as we moved further inland, and in open areas of sand between stands of vegetation we discovered piles of small and medium-sized rocks clustered in such a way to resemble awkward pyramids, and none of these appeared accidental. Our geologist drew our attention to the fact that he had seen no large rocks since we had landed and then he suggested that any large rocks on the island could have been intentionally reduced in size. As we moved forward we speculated about how these stone clusters might be interpreted. From the elaborations of their sandcastles we recognized that these ghosts must possess exceptional manual skills, but with these pyramids we needed to consider their physical strength as well. How, we wondered, could ectoplasmic creatures move hard and heavy objects? Although sand may appear intentionally shaped, its grains will move with the lightest breeze and accident will result in unlikely shapes. Despite, or perhaps because of, the range of our academic backgrounds we found ourselves uncomfortable about our confusion. So on the possibility these stone piles hid something we might recognize, our geologist disassembled one, but at its bottom he found nothing. As an experiment we decided to leave these stones scattered and return later to see if they had been moved or otherwise additionally disturbed.

Further on, we came upon a small shack just taller than a man assembled from sections of rough driftwood and irregular pieces of tin and with a small glass window. Instantly we were curious. The structure appeared imperfectly shaped and awkwardly made and did not seem to be occupied, but we resisted moving close; the sand immediately around its entrance was pristine and free from marks or indentations and we decided this would be valuable to our research. Instead, we speculated from our distance about who might have built it and why. Although the shack appeared to be a sort of shelter, this island lay at a considerable distance from its closest neighbors and so it seemed unlikely it had been visited by those neighbors even at long intervals. Otherwise, none of us could conjure a reason a ghost might build such a thing, despite those manual skills and the physical strength they apparently possessed. Several of us speculated the shack might be some form of trap and that these ghosts planned an unpleasant surprise for that human foolish enough to enter. But at least in this instance we confronted the question of intention.

Circling around the shack, we continued toward the center of the island and discovered a gradual rise in the land that led to a broad plateau. We were surprised we had not recognized this from the ship. In contrast to the portion of the island we had crossed, this plateau was thickly covered with small trees and broad bushes all growing tightly together and suggesting something that resembled a garden.

Calling a halt to our survey as the sun approached the horizon, we agreed to pitch our tents and remain on the island overnight. In our preparation for landing we had made certain that in addition to our tents we had carried sufficient supplies. Unlike the terrain closer to the beach, the trees and bushes around us here were so tightly clustered we realized we would need to cut many down in order to pitch our tents close together.

Those of us who did not take up tools began to sort through our supplies preparing to establish our camp. So we were all surprised when the first ax struck the first tree to hear a sudden though very quiet groan. Confident this could only be coincidence, the sounds of hacking and chopping around us soon were loud. Near the center of our cleared space we built a small fire which we fed with the limbs of the vegetation we cut down along with armloads of the debris of dead and dried limbs.

As we set up our tents we discovered that an acrid and bad-smelling smoke had begun to billow from our fire. At first we assumed it was the result of the freshly-cut fuel and that eventually it would dissipate. We did not realize that our voyage's darkest chapter had already begun.

The smoke became less dense although its foul odor seemed to grow stronger until eventually we worried that its terrible smell would permeate our food and make it inedible. But night was approaching and we were all very hungry, so eventually we braved it. Just as we feared, that dank odor flavored our food but it did not prove to be as obnoxious as we had feared. Heartened by our meal and with so much work confronting us for the next day, we looked forward to a solid night's sleep.

After a time of quiet breathing, the whisper of a cool breeze from the sea was all that could be heard. But first one and then another of us began to make sounds as we slept; feeble moans mixed with weak cries of distress so that eventually similar sounds came from every tent. Our dispiriting chorus continued through the night.

When the sun arose we emerged from our tents wide-eyed and confused as if startled by what we saw since in our dreams we had come to assume we would awake somewhere else. We sat around the fire for a time with our heads in our hands struggling to disentangle what we believed from what we knew. One of us stirred our fire awake and then assembled something that resembled a meal. Once again the fire's pungent smoke surrounded us, but we were all so bleary we ate and drank whatever was placed before us.

It was well into the morning before finally we began to speak, and then it was as if a dam within each of us had broken. Suddenly we each were eager to describe what we had experienced during the night. Almost simultaneously, each of us conjectured weird and obscure locations and strangely sequenced scenes where people we had known but in no way recognized gestured flailing desperately in some indecipherable but frantic attempt to communicate something to us as if in possession of the most urgent message. Our voices as we reported what we recalled were pinched with concern and several of us spoke with tears in our eyes.

Suddenly we saw the ship's first-mate approaching us from the beach and this startled us. When he reached us he asked if there was something wrong, and his question as much as his visit left us confused. When asked what had brought him to us he replied that the Captain had recognized signs of our distress and so had dispatched him to give us help.

We looked at each other surprised. We conceded our anxious night to the first-mate but none of us recalled having sent a distress signal. We assured him we had never believed we were in physical danger. And in any case it was unclear how he or the Captain could have helped us.

Despite our assurances the first-mate appeared annoyed when we insisted we were fine. Perhaps something in our response or our demeanor struck him as frivolous and led him to offer to remain on the island with us. Although we repeated our assurance, his expression remained concerned but after some hesitation he returned to the ship.

All of this prevented us from resuming our survey until nearly mid-day. We agreed to revisit the site of the disassembled pyramid to test the geologist's hypothesis that it was an intentional creation since this might tell us something about our ghosts. While it seemed an intriguing hypothesis, several of us questioned whether anything useful could be revealed one way or the other. But simple curiosity led even our skeptics to join us. When we reached the cluster of stones what we found left us silent.

That pyramid we had disassembled remained as we recalled it, but each of the other pyramids close by had also been disassembled and their stones had been scattered in a way that resembled the pattern of the one we had disassembled. Our reaction instantly was to attempt a hypothesis, because what we found left us thoroughly confounded. More than the question of how these pyramids could have been taken apart, the most compelling question again seemed to be intention; why had this been done? What question were these scatters of stone assumed to answer? We had no doubt these pyramids had been left intact the day before, so unless this was the work of the first-mate, their disturbance could only have occurred during our agitated evening.

It seemed intuitively true that some relationship existed between the ghosts and these stones, and now we found we needed to question that relationship. Our geologist reassembled the structure he had disassembled the previous day to see if any stones had been added or removed. Meanwhile our botanist speculated that all of these disassemblies had been contrived to appear identical because whoever had disassembled the other pyramids was convinced that it had been our intentional creation, just as we had assumed the pyramids were the intentional creations of the ghosts. While this appeared plausible, we were confused as to how we might elaborate her speculation.

Perhaps due to our frustration or simply the result of our disparate skills, it was our meteorologist who offered an intriguing suggestion. She proposed that we could only recognize the intention of these ghosts after we identified their method of communicating their thoughts to each other. As subtle as this suggestion appeared, none of us was able to describe a strategy likely either to confirm or contradict its possibility. As our geologist asked, how did we know that these ghosts did not communicate by some ghostly telepathy? Our unanimous decision then was to resist conclusions and continue our survey. We decided to walk the circumference of the plateau in search of additional stone pyramids and particularly to determine if any remained intact. This demanded several hours yet each of the pyramids we found had been reduced to a scatter of stones.

But to our surprise and confusion we found that, in the time it took for us to walk around the island, the previously disassembled pyramid had been rebuilt. And even more baffling, other pyramids which we had found disassembled remained so. This appeared to deny any pattern we assumed we recognized and left us utterly confused and uncertain even of our memories. But in another inspired intuition, our botanist suggested that we return to our campsite; whoever had been active among these piles of stones may also have made mischief there. Paranoia then circulated among us like a bad cold so we hurried back to our campsite.

Surprised in part by our lack of surprise, we found that where we had cut down vegetation in a limited area, all of the vegetation to the edge of the plateau had been cut down, and in just the way we had done it. We considered how briefly we had been away and had to assume this could only have been accomplished by a small army of ghosts.

At this point each thing we found inscrutable we attributed to these ghosts. Our botanist suggested that they were both intrigued and annoyed by us, and what we saw was their ambivalent response to our presence. Once again we wrestled with the question of how ghosts might communicate their intentions. Our meteorologist then put forward an interesting speculation. She reminded us that we had assumed these ghosts are the spirits of those who have lived before, with personal histories and individual identities. But suppose these are ghosts of beings who were doomed never to live and therefore never acquire histories or individual identities? What if their ghostly existence is the only form of existence they can ever possess and that they are aware of this and perhaps even a bit resentful? Is it possible they observe us hoping to learn how we live and adopting what they perceive as our persona? In short, she wondered if they had observed our actions and then engaged in those activities they observed all with the conviction that in this way they would achieve existence.

Her speculation stunned all of us. At that moment we recognized ourselves as hobbled by, and all but entombed within, thoughtlessly conventional thinking. We had not scrutinized what we had observed, but instead struggled merely to force our observations into those forms we already knew and found comfortable. Perhaps, she suggested, we simply needed to allow these ghosts to observe and then imitate us. We could then follow their choices to understand what these attempts revealed about them.

Even those of us intrigued by this suggestion were confused by how to bring it about. We looked around our campsite and then further off, to that vegetation cut down somehow and by hands apparently other than our own. In response to this challenge our meteorologist suggested we rearrange portions of that vegetation which we assumed had been cut down by our ghosts, but in some way which was meaningful to us. A baffled silence followed, until our botanist suggested that each of us weave some of the thin branches of the vegetation into crude baskets. When questioned, she suggested that since none of us were expert at making baskets, each of us would construct a noticeably different basket, and that if any of these were reproduced by the ghosts we would recognize that instantly.

None of us had a more pertinent suggestion to offer and the meteorologist's proposal provided something worth considering as well as something to do.

We began this exercise of making baskets with the hope of proving our hypothesis, but quickly it became clear that some of us enjoyed it. By the time twilight approached each of us had made several baskets, and as our meteorologist had surmised, even those made by the same person were noticeably different. We then arranged them on the ground beside each other in a circle to surround our campsite. We had no idea how many ghosts were on the island but we hoped to provide each a challenge.

As evening descended we rebuilt our fire and prepared our meal. That peculiar odor surrounded us again and flavored our food but we had become skilled at ignoring it. Having spent so much time making those baskets we were intensely curious about what might result. Night fell with a thrilling promise of revelation the following morning.

And perhaps because of our excitement we again slept fitfully. Whether our nighttime whimpers and groans became loud enough to alert our Captain was a question none of us could answer. We were each too busy wrestling with that apparently real world which descended upon us behind our closed eyes. A storm may have passed over us, there may have been thunder and lightning accompanied by heavy rain and strong wind, and perhaps one of us even became separated from our camp and briefly lost. Encased within that density of night, bemused within its quagmire of darkness, buffeted by that slipstream of migrating spirits, none of us remained alert enough to remember all of whatever we were certain we had seen and heard. The images conjured within our minds remained as real as those crude baskets we had made.

But the sun eventually rose, our new day arrived, and like children at Christmas morning we left our tents eager to see what had been left for us. And none of our speculations prepared us for what we found and we could neither believe nor understand what we saw.

In place of those baskets we had placed at the edge of our campsite, we found twigs and sticks carefully laid on the ground parallel to each other and all following that curve demarcating the circle around our campsite. We were baffled at first by the question of where these twigs and sticks could have come from, and even more confused by the question of why our baskets had been removed and these had been put in their place and within that peculiar configuration. We speculated for a time but then our botanist knelt to look more closely at the sticks and twigs. After another moment she stood shaking her head and with a startled voice announced that she recognized those twigs she had used to construct her baskets. Someone among us laughed as if certain the botanist had made a joke. But the rest of us moved to where we each remembered having placed our baskets and our curiosity turned to shock.

During the night each of our baskets had been disassembled, reduced to their parts, and then those parts had been arranged into parallel lines which followed the outline of their original placement. This discovery caused all of us to forget any appetite for breakfast.

Even after we recognized those twigs we each had used to make our baskets, nothing we saw suggested how we might understand this. And worst of all, nothing suggested what we should do next. What we saw appeared to be a clue to something, but what it suggested or how we should understand it was invisible to us. Without knowing what question had been asked we could not recognize how we should understand this response.

Baffled by what we found, we must have presented a scene of exceptional confusion to the first-mate as he once again approached our camp. When finally he reached us he looked around and then began to laugh, perhaps as much out of embarrassment as confusion. He asked casually what had happened. By putting our confusion into words his question fell as a physical blow. What appeared to have happened seemed so unlikely that none of us could describe what we suspected. Then, with a forced good-humor, our botanist asked the first-mate if on his journey to reach us he had seen anyone inside the shack. He responded with mild surprise by asking what shack she was referring to. With this our confusion turned to concern.

Our meteorologist was the first to volunteer to go and take a look, but instantly the rest of us joined her. We reached the location of where we all remembered having seen that shack, except that we found nothing. Even its parts and all of the marks it had made in the sand were gone. To this point we had been confused about what was going on around us, but now we were frightened. Meanwhile, our botanist finally asked the first-mate what had led him to repeat his visit, and he replied that the Captain this time had been certain we were in danger and had sent him to help us. At that moment we realized we needed to communicate directly somehow with these ghosts.

Instinctively we turned to the botanist since she had come up with the notion of making baskets. But she looked around as baffled as the rest of us.

Despite our confusion we were compelled to conjecture. And our first question was to what possible purpose a shack would be built only to disappear. What had been communicated by that action? We had assumed our investigation would answer the questions we had arrived with, but to this point we merely accumulated questions without solutions. The first-mate walked away with an odd smile shaking his head and offering the hope we would soon sort all of this out. None of us shared his optimism.

Events had taken place, objects had moved or been moved as if according to some consciousness possessing a plan and yet we had no intuition concerning any intention behind these actions. Even more disturbing, we were unable to imagine how any of all of this had been physically accomplished. Since we first landed we had seen no footprints other than our own, so we lacked the evidence even to surmise that what we had found was the result of conscious intention. And while our research involved material resources within a material environment, that material we had encountered told us nothing. How could ectoplasim modify material unless ectoplasim possessed materiality? And if that was so, did that mean that ectoplasim itself was merely another form of that material making up the universe? And if that was so, what in the end was immaterial? Although we had conceded that they existed, our ghosts refused to communicate but they also refused to leave us alone.

What had begun in optimism had degenerated into one simple question; was there any way to seduce these vaporous creatures into exposing themselves, to making themselves available for interrogation and justifying their actions? And if they could not be seduced, how otherwise might they be compelled to respond? For a moment we turned to our botanist whose intuitions had proved so intriguing and waited for her to offer a path other than surrender and flight.

After a moment she said there was one experiment we had not performed which might yield useful results. With that she turned and began to walk back to the campsite, and the rest of us followed.

There she disappeared into her tent for a moment and then reappeared with her bag of instruments. She sat down beside our smoldering camp fire and from her bag brought out a glass slide. She held the slide flat and low over a patch of the fire still yielding smoke and the slide quickly became covered with black soot. She set that aside and brought out a bottle closed with an eyedropper cap. Using the cap she placed two drops of the fluid inside the bottle onto the soot-covered slide. The nearly-colorless liquid quickly turned pale pink and then red, but then suddenly blue for a moment before turning green. The botanist then looked around nodding, as if to say that she should have known.

But seated on his knapsack some distance from the fire, our anthropologist suddenly spoke up and asked about those sandcastles. He had been dutiful and helpful to our survey and had assisted whenever asked, but having discovered no human remains to analyze he had remained on the periphery of our survey. We all turned quizzically in his direction. He reminded us that we had discovered those sandcastles long before we built the fire. While the rest of us pondered his observation, he stood saying he wanted to take a walk on the beach. Before he had gone very far the rest of us stood and followed.

Passing the spot where we all remembered having seen the shack, our anthropologist casually reminded us that we had seen that long before building the fire as well.

As we approached the beach, to our surprise we spied the first-mate and several sailors standing beside their beached longboat. Reaching the beach we found that an exceptionally high tide had come in and all of the sandcastles were gone. We said nothing as the first-mate stepped away from his longboat to join us.

He smiled as he announced that he was relieved to see us since it meant he would not need to search the entire island to find us. This certainly confused us since we all remembered his earlier visits. When asked, he said he had come from the Captain who had decided it was long past time that our team prepared to leave. His announcement left us baffled. With a suddenly surprised expression he looked around at all of us before announcing that we had already been on this island eight days and then wondered aloud how much longer we needed to remain.

Our expressions apparently betrayed our disbelief because he turned to the meteorologist and asked how long we thought we had been on the island. Without answering we asked him and his sailors to accompany us back to our camp to help us pack and carry our belongings.

We headed back across the beach and discovered that a dozen paces beyond the water's edge our footprints disappeared. The first-mate turned to us scratching his head and asked from which direction we had come. We did not respond as we continued toward our campsite. The geologist muttered a comment about the absence of the stone pyramids which none of us felt confident enough to respond to. Eventually we reached what we remembered as our campsite.

To our astonishment we found that every bit of vegetation we had cut down had re-grown and the entire site reformed into that thick stand of vegetation we recalled when we arrived. No cut limbs cluttered the ground, no charred remains of our camp fire smoldered or lay about cold. In fact, every sign of disturbance that indicated we had camped there had disappeared. But most startling and most frightening, our tents, our supplies and every piece of our equipment all had been disassembled and then neatly packed up, and their bundles then had been tidily stacked into a small pyramid. The first-mate turned to us asking how we had guessed that he would be arriving soon to retrieve us.

There seemed nothing left to be done, so we returned with the first-mate to our ship and moved on.

ISLAND OF WANDERING SHADOWS

THE GROUP OF NINE ISLANDS formed a scattered archipelago whose outline on our map resembled a diamond, and that island among them which we planned to survey was recorded as having been visited by a fourteenth-century explorer. Our assignment was to uncover evidence of the explorer and any members of his crew who had been buried there. Most of the relevant documents disappeared long ago but those that remained convinced us traces of that explorer's visit remained and would not be difficult to locate. We hoped to find evidence to overturn a common speculation that upon reaching the island the crew was met with hostility from an uncertain source after which they mutinied and the explorer and several members of his crew were murdered. The documents alleged that their bodies remained on the island.

So when as we approached the island it began to rain we were confident this could be no worse than an inconvenience. And later when the storm became fierce we remained confident the skill of our Captain would keep us safe. And that likely would have happened had a sailor not failed to tie down one of the lines of the ship's rigging.

With the strength and duration of the storm, his failure drove our ship onto an outcropping of rocks just beyond the island's breakers and the impact fractured planks of our hull allowing sea water into the hold. Our Captain assigned his crew to the pumps but the storm became stronger and despite their efforts our ship began to list to one side. He said nothing about our danger, but our experienced colleagues muttered that capsize was something we were unlikely to survive. Anxiety kept us alert through the night but when finally the storm weakened we were able to anchor close to the island. This allowed us to begin our survey while the ship's crew began repairs.

According to a brief account written by one of the survivors of the explorer's voyage, a week before they reached this island their ship ran out of fresh water so that when finally they dropped anchor the crew barely had sufficient strength to row to shore. And despite their relief and optimism, upon landing they found only small pools of standing water, foul-smelling, cloudy and infested with insects. Bitter words were exchanged and the explorer's life was threatened. The account then offered praise to God because shortly after sunset, a violent yet revivifying rain storm suddenly caught up with them.

This archipelago lay along the trade winds where powerful storms were frequent and the collection of that storm's rainwater saved most of the crew from death, but unfortunately not all. Their ship had reached the island in poor condition and the crew needed to recover their strength before they could begin repairs. So according to the fragment, resigned to remaining on the island for a length of time, the crew built a small camp comprised of a single large lean-to of branches and palm-fronds lashed together and then surrounded it with a palisade of palm tree trunks. This provided their shelter for more than a month. But the fragment failed to explain what danger compelled them to make these constructions and we hoped to answer that question as well.

Our team was concerned, first, to find evidence of the palisade's existence along with its dimensions. Fortification suggested necessity in response to serious threat and we could only assume it had been built in response to the presence of inhabitants hostile to their arrival. The account alluded to inhabitants but the description of their decorations and actions were so wildly dissimilar that historians regarded these as confused and ignorant hyperbole. But we hoped to locate artifacts of those inhabitants and perhaps reconstruct that contact. In addition to remains of the palisade, we hoped to locate and recover any remains of the buried sailors along with material they left behind.

After the departure of the explorer's ship and what remained of its crew, the island was visited only twice more, and the most recent more than one hundred and fifty years before. The account of that visit reported stone and wood remains which were assumed evidence of the earlier explorer's presence.

However, that account did not mention inhabitants and this suggested that at some moment either they had abandoned the island or had been compelled to flee. Legends among the inhabitants of the neighboring islands offered confusing accounts of conflicts among various islanders which we hoped also to sort out.

A small group from our team traveled to the island early that first day to conduct a general survey, and when its members returned to our ship they were especially excited by their discovery of roughly-shaped stones within a perimeter of decayed stumps of palm trees. They agreed these seemed to resemble those remains we hoped to find. Our chemist acting as our team's leader spoke confidently that once our entire group reached the island we would quickly collect the artifacts and data that would provide evidence to clarify those accounts.

Over our mid-day meal the Captain, who usually remained aloof from our conversation as though satisfied simply to assure our safe arrival, became expansive and shared with us a rumor he had heard about our island. According to this, following the last visit a century and a half before, captains regularly steered clear of the island. No captain would admit this but its pattern was so consistent it seemed impossible it could be accidental.

The leader of our team explained to the Captain that the few surviving documents included many gaps. While some pages had rotted or had been torn accidentally, others appeared to have been removed intentionally. With a smile the Captain agreed there was a great deal of misinformation about the island, and assured her that correcting that information justified our journey. He then speculated that some deletions had been made in order to keep the island's location secret and this for economic reasons, while tales of mysterious and threatening forces had been added to discourage curiosity. All of that, he continued, suggested there was something significant and perhaps valuable on the island. Our leader admitted she would be delighted if that proved to be the case since we would be the first to describe and analyze it. Our Captain then reminded her that the price of curiosity is rarely its cost. After a long moment of thoughtful silence someone asked about Stanley.

Our leader looked about as if certain the man sat nearby, but then her expression became puzzled. The rest of us turned confident he sat among us. When one of our team asked if she had seen Stanley board the longboat, she nodded with instant certainty. But then she looked sheepishly away and the rest of us uncomfortably did the same.

Someone asked if it was possible Stanley had failed to return to the longboat and now stood on the beach waving his arms and calling out that he had been abandoned. We stood from the table and returned to the deck and looked to the beach but saw no one there. After a moment of embarrassed silence, under the bright sun and glancing to the island it became clear that none of us was certain who Stanley was. We insisted we had seen him during the voyage but as we questioned each other, even his role as a member of our team appeared uncertain. And then one among us asked what exactly Stanley had looked like. The thick silence that followed enveloped all of us and left us even more embarrassed than confused.

Speculation erupted. Questions and responses multiplied as they divided until we were forced to admit that no two of us remembered the same person. None of us agreed at which university he had taught, or what books or journal articles he had published, what his course of study had been or even what language he spoke. Finally, the Captain asked the only question none of us was prepared to ask; were we certain that a person named Stanley had traveled with us? A darker silence was our response and despite the sultry climate it chilled us all.

Our leader suggested the Captain review his list of passengers while our geologist went below determined to identify Stanley's bunk and belongings. In the end we were startled to discover that we found no material evidence a person named Stanley had been aboard our ship. And yet for a reason none of us could articulate we remained certain he had made this journey with us. Several insisted they remembered having spoken with him, and at least two claimed they had watched him climb into the longboat. But without evidence, every question remained unresolved. Finally we confronted the question of whether we would suspend our survey and search for someone we were uncertain existed.

We were intrigued by the island's mysteries but our most urgent question now was whether we had abandoned a member of our team named Stanley on that island. And despite our other conjectures we failed to ask whether he might not be alone.

Our Captain paced the deck with an expression that was both dubious and annoyed. By now we were all eager to return to the island and search for Stanley. And we were relieved when he ordered the first-mate to gather a search party and launch the longboat. He spoke as though determined to resolve the question of this missing man and quickly.

He asked if the reconnaissance team had identified evidence in addition to those mysterious stones that might suggest humans currently inhabited the island. When no one responded he shook his head in disbelief. He then ordered the first-mate to take command of the ship because he personally would direct our search for Stanley. To the rest of us he announced that if Stanley remained on the island, he could not be alone. Silently we each began to wonder how concerned we should be.

As we rowed back to the island, the Captain recounted a tale he had heard which claimed that the inhabitants of this island possessed the ability to confuse human minds, and that they employed this power whenever strangers approached. Acknowledging that this could only be preposterous, he reminded us that just such a tale could account for the avoidance by other captains of the island. He then suggested this also explained our experiences, because somehow we found ourselves deeply confused about Stanley. How these inhabitants might accomplish this confusion he was unable even to guess, but he cautioned us all to remain alert. When we asked what we should look for, he smiled promising we would know it when we saw it.

Upon landing we encountered our first puzzle. Footprints in the sand made by our earlier landing remained clear, but then our survey's leader insisted other footprints had been added; there were, she said, many more now than she remembered. We wondered if any were Stanley's. But when asked, she was unable to distinguish those she believed had been added.

The Captain asked again if anything we had seen beyond those mysterious upright stones and stumps of palms the first team had found could be evidence of inhabitants and our silence appeared to provoke him. He insisted that unless we could be certain of this we would need to search the entire island. This discouraged us, but at least it offered a plan likely to answer our questions. We began our search by following the beach and about half-way around the island we discovered marks in the sand resembling human footprints but at a location we were certain none of us had visited. Their clusters were separated by unblemished areas of sand and these defeated every speculation, particularly the possibility they had been made by Stanley.

When our circuit of the island finally was complete, aside from those peculiar footprints we found nothing we suspected had been made by humans. The Captain listened to our conjectures although it seemed he heard none that were useful. Convinced we needed to move toward the interior of the island we pushed ahead through vegetation that was surprisingly dense. But a short distance beyond the beach we found those stones and stumps the earlier visit had identified. The stones appeared to have been intentionally propped upright and the stumps bore what resembled carved figures which could have been symbols or even images. None of us offered a guess at their meaning. The Captain did not ask but clearly he wondered why we could not account for what we found. To complicate this question further, the smooth shapes of the stone figures almost appeared the result of natural erosion. We conjectured that they had been carved and then, as some gesture of sacrifice to a deity unknown to us, intentionally abandoned to the powers of nature. We hoped this mystery was separate from that involving Stanley.

But how does one meaningfully speculate about a person who may not exist? Unlike questions concerning the existence of habitable planets which are resolved through probabilities based on the laws of chemistry and physics, what principles make it more or less likely that a particular human named Stanley exists? Humans might or might not inhabit this island but no principle in natural science makes a human named Stanley either more or less likely to be among them. He seemed to hover in that discomforted space of remembered dream where the simple effort to recall erases that memory. Our convictions about him might be nothing more than conjectures, fluid, shapeless and unstable, so that every assertion dissolved into fog.

The Captain, meanwhile, suggested that if there was any truth to the legend, beings able to confuse us and thereby make themselves invisible surrounded us observing us and listening to us and determined to reach conclusions. Moving beyond those stone figures we continued toward the center of the island, and although we saw neither Stanley nor any other sign of these inhabitants, we continued to find inscrutable footprints.

As we searched we began to notice signs of another approaching storm. We asked the Captain whether we should seek shelter, but before he could respond the sky clouded so suddenly it was as if we had all blinked simultaneously to discover overhead a dense gray and billowing blanket. What began to fall as droplets resembling a heavy mist soon became rain. Finally we needed to find shelter. In the storm's deepening twilight those rain drops grew large as they fell faster with a hissing roar. Enwrapped by the rain we tried to look about, but in its diminishing light those shadows around us merely became deeper.

We wandered half-blinded through the thickening rain until suddenly we recognized a shallow grotto opening from the side of a low hill. It appeared sufficiently broad and high and we moved under its shelter hopeful the rain would soon end. But the rain had to fall even heavier and our liquid darkness become even thicker before suddenly we began to see them.

What we saw at first more resembled shadows within even darker shadows. The weak glitter of falling rain passed through these shadows and as it did so each drop momentarily sparkled like a tiny sliver of glass so that the shapes of these shadows appeared as flicking contours of fragile and fragmented light. These shadows gradually took on human shapes and moved as if annoyed by our presence although they remained close by. Had Stanley also seen these as well and was he now hiding somewhere from them? We turned to the Captain admitting that despite his promise we had no idea what we were seeing or what it meant nor what we should do next. Deafened now by the roar of the storm our Captain pointed to these shadows insisting this was the opportunity we said we had hoped for and we should act. But in that darkness we were confused and wet and nothing made sense.

As these shadows of scintillating light drifted across the entrance to our grotto, occasionally one or another turned in our direction as if looking at us, although those spaces where there should have been eyes were cast into such darkness we could only surmise their gaze. Were their movements as aimless as they appeared or were they following a plan; we could not even guess. The rain fell now driven by blasts of wind which sent it sideways into our eyes. By their postures these shadows appeared perplexed and curious; moving within darkness they paused as if intrigued but uncertain as if suspecting that something important was before them if only they could recognize it. They seemed never to speak or gesture to each other and in fact moved about as if aware of but uninterested in any others. And unsurprisingly, they left no footprints. So one question we hoped we had answered simply became deeper.

Uncertain how to proceed, we were trapped within the quagmire of our unresolved curiosity. The rain now fell in waves so dense it resembled a cascade. The shadows clustered together standing nearly shoulder to shoulder and peering down. To our surprise and despite our ignorance of how all of this could be, we recognized suddenly that what moved before us and what we watched were shadows and not ghosts.

This was less a conclusion than a firm intuition, like confronting someone in a darkened room only to discover one's own image reflected from an unexpected mirror. A certitude inexplicably derived, we knew there could be nothing mystical about these beings since they were not beings at all. Ghosts are composed of some ghostly substance whereas these shadows were gaps like the absence of light, spaces in that material continuum within which we all swim. We could neither explain nor describe under what circumstances such after-images could come into being or continue to exist. No hypothesis seemed adequate to encompass such ephemerality. They existed only as absence rather than presence. What we perceived were vacancies, replacements, place-holders for that which had once existed. Philosophers had debated the existence of such resonant beings and here we were, certain of what we were seeing yet helpless to identify material evidence of that which could only be immaterial. We did not attempt to explain this. We recognized that these shadows could only be those resonant echoes of the previously occupied spaces of the presence of those people who had preceded them. And it seemed certain to us that these were not those core entities or super-subtle beings which remain and endure as unified selves which abide beyond death.

Having reached this recognition it was suddenly obvious that the shadows confronting us included, among others, those of the explorer and his crew. And looking further into the darkness we recognized those resonant images of other humans who had set foot on this island. As best we could surmise, these shadows recapitulated in brief those actions and behaviors of their originals. We pondered the possibility we were observing an alternative form of fate; an unresolved form of existence whereby their originals remained free to move about while these shadows were condemned to this island repeating past gestures and retracing previous steps and for all eternity.

The rain now fell in sheets that varied with an irregular tempo. These shadows did not rise and fall in any rhythmic counterpoint but appeared to move in a subtle harmony to the rain's discontinuous rhythm. We were charmed by this subtle movement, a series of barely-perceptible gestures we somehow perceived and found delicious to follow. With our attentions utterly compromised we could not look away but eventually, finally, we recognized that Stanley was not among them.

Of course none of this precisely amounted to recognition. Since these shadows had no distinctive shape to distinguish them from each other, we could not explain how we knew this but we were certain that Stanley was not among them and just as certain he never had been. Surprisingly, this intuition was simultaneous among all of us, firm and absolute though unspoken. Its certainty was not based on our agreement about Stanley's appearance, an impossibility since we had no specific memory of the man, and these shadows provided no clue. So perhaps, like our recognition of these as shadows rather than as ghosts, it was simply because we could not justify our certainty that it was unshakable. We were now confident he had never visited this island but a more urgent difficulty occurred to us. Had there ever been an original Stanley?

Absent his shadow here and belongings on the ship, where exactly was Stanley, if he existed at all? More perplexing, could it ever be the case that a shadow replaced its original? Every shadow, like every reflection, depends on something previously-existent. We could only watch closely and hope that one of these shadows would betray something useful to us. Gradually the rain became so heavy it threatened to flood our grotto and drive us out. But for as long as we were able, we scrutinized these shadows optimistic that something more was about to become clear. Our perplexity remained complete, however, and even more impenetrable than the darkness surrounding us.

Then, for the first time since the rain had begun to fall, a bolt of lightning split the sky accompanied by a deafening explosion. Having stared so long into the glittering darkness we were all simultaneously blinded and deafened. For that instant we stood together separately, each of us within that shelter suddenly and utterly alone and unaware of any other near us. In this way we recognized that those other, more distant, shadows were ourselves. Perplexed, we watched what we became convinced were ourselves wandering within those moments which had already passed but also in those moments which had not yet passed but would do so eventually, inscribing on the air an echo, a resonance, of our presence.

We watched as those moments of future and present superimposed over each other so that the past would endure saturated within the present as an irresolvable residue of each of us moving, advancing and retreating, and all simultaneously within this fated space and transpiring within this time. These shadows repeated our movements in the only way those moments were retained within the island's memory, presences even more ephemeral than footprints. From this we concluded that those footprints we had seen were fragments of the island's flawed and incomplete memory, echoes of the passages of all those who had already stepped, and would eventually step, onto this island. We speculated that this imperfection of the island's memory explained the irregular and unlikely placement of the footprints, just as it explained the absence of features for the shadows. So we were compelled to wonder if this explained the absence of Stanley; had the island simply forgotten him and thereby eliminated even his shadow? And then it occurred to us that it was possible the explorer and his sailors had also seen these shadows but without understanding them, and that this was what had driven them to build their palisade eager to protect themselves from these inexplicable but undoubtedly demonic creatures.

Within that darkness and under that pouring rain we recognized ourselves watching our own shadows, and in some instances several shadows of ourselves, each separated by time, sometimes moments, sometimes years. The downpour continued while we struggled to see further into the distance. We could not see as clearly or as far as we wished, but we recognized that the terrain before us was dense with moving shadows and far more of them than we had at first recognized. These shadows, the echoes of every presence, could only be the permanent though incomplete images lodged in the island's memory and which would remain so within every future. In this way and like the explorer and his ship's crew, we will always remain visiting this island.

Eventually the rain weakened and then passed. We stepped out from under the shelter of the grotto as the sun began to peek through torn steel-gray clouds. The shadows were no longer visible, but we were compelled to assume they remained close by, moving and observing. We looked to the Captain, but he simply shrugged and then turned to begin our retreat to the beach and to our ship.

But we suspected that finally we had resolved our questions concerning Stanley; first and foremost we confirmed that whether he had been with us he had never visited this island, nor would he in any future. This conclusion provided us with something resembling relief even while it told us nothing about the man's current state of existence. As well, by these shadows we were assured of the presence of the explorer and his crew so that it was merely necessary to locate whatever material evidence of them remained. Because those shadows could only exist if their original beings had existed, and having existed, material evidence of their existence must also exist. With this guarantee we were eager to gather that evidence which must exist and complete our investigation, confident now that such material remains inevitably would be found. And also because we were certain finally that although this island might forget, it could neither invent nor could it remember that which had not occurred.

ISLAND OF FALSE DREAMS

ON THIS DEVIOUS AND DECEPTIVE ISLAND we remained awake and it was our furious dreams which kept us awake.

That is, our dreams were so vivid, so haunting and enigmatic, that we could never be certain when we slept. But when our dreams merged and blended, our deepest danger was that our unique worlds had fragmented and their fragments had become jumbled and confused. Uncertain of everything including our uncertainty, we were compelled to sort through those fragments of dream and hope to distinguish each from every other which defined our selves. Within this confluence of fragmentary selves we made choices never certain where any dream or its dreamer ended or began. For whom was a particular fragment of a particular dream its dreamer's reality? As their authors we writhed in uneasy wakefulness with only dreams and their echoes our ignorant guides and devious companions.

We had arrived at this island and its towering volcano with a systematic plan to explore its most pungent secrets. Our intention was honorable and strategy well-formed; our geologist, our meteorologist, our oceanographer and our anthropologist were each eager to begin although with distinctly different expectations. We made this journey only after much study and were confident of at least a few facts concerning the island. But when our longboat reached the shore, even that little which we believed we knew fell away like a dissipating fog as insufficient if not deviant. Meanwhile, from the beginning of our journey our first-mate, a slim man of advanced but indeterminate age and wearing a black patch, had been suspicious of this voyage and its ambitions. Only much later would we learn why.

The evening of our arrival and riding at anchor in the island's lagoon our dreams became so vivid and distinctive they overlaid the island with uncountable alternative islands. Each particular dream arose and expanded as a cloud within a deeper darkness of roiling and billowing dreams possessing ephemeral tendrils so that even sequence itself became a speculation whose path remained impossible to distinguish. At the center of each dream, recognized events became obscure and irretrievable, instantly suggesting alternative realities residing dissolved within that which we had been certain was a dream.

We all agreed that at one moment we stood on the deck of our ship under a uneven blanket of ash-gray clouds, listening to our Captain describe our challenges and their dangers, but then some inscrutable moments later we stood under the hot sun on the island's bright pale beach watching wet oars glisten as our longboat retreated to our ship and we turned to advance toward our island's interior. At that moment we were certain that our Captain was a tall and slim-built man, except for those of us who dreamed him small and more round; several of us dreamed the first-mate as young and fresh-faced, while others dreamed him gray, limping and grizzled. And some of us recalled having set off from gloomy Bristol, except for those of us certain we had departed from sultry Alexandria.

Perched on its furthest edge we dreamed our island was so broad and high it would demand hours to circumnavigate and climb, except for those dreaming a flat, yellow island as featureless as mist and hardly larger than a hope. An island some dreamed as lush with vegetation appeared to others as disguised by pale and sparkling crusts of salt that sheathed its rocky rubble. On this island which we agreed was uninhabited we dreamed beings so variously shaped and structured and hued they could have arrived at any time from anywhere, unless also nowhere and at no time. Given our divergent certainties and how awkwardly they failed to blend into our dreams, it was inevitable that in the end it was these variegated inhabitants which intrigued us and seduced us as the ultimate objects of speculation.

While each of us insisted that this and only this had happened, none of us recalled those moments and their details as recalled by others, and so none of us possessed every piece of our island's puzzle. It appeared to be in the nature of this island that possession of any single bit of information about it demanded abandonment of another.

We assured each other that all of this must finally sort itself out; dreams, we insisted to ourselves as well as each other, could not simply fold into other dreams into infinity. The bottom of every dream beyond which nothing more could be dreamed must be reached. Every descent into dream must reach a moment within which everything beyond fades into the darkness of reality. But despite loud insistence, even this recognition eluded most of us much of the time.

We struggled to rouse ourselves from a psychic lethargy, our mental somnolence, but every effort failed, or at least appeared so within our dreams. That is, the seams in that fabric which bound our dreams together never became distinct, even with the subtlest caress of our memories or the softest breath from our eyes. Ghosts of those seams, their folds and edges, emerged in a hazy glow of muted colors, but even that sensation of recognizing ectoplasmic boundaries seemed itself a dream which evaporated in a moment. Although we could not know it then, within our conflated dreams we were about to learn true fear.

We agreed that once we had stood together on the deck of our ship, but later we stood together on the scintillating sand of the beach. Every inflection between those moments fled past our inner eyes like the contents of a box of shattered glass tossed into the air. These dreams nesting within dreams and each collapsing into the next baffled us, until it appeared that exploration of our island had itself finally dissolved into fantasies of exploration. Each of our dreamed islands threatened to emerge inscrutable within every dream of each dreamer. But even confused within these dreams we pushed forward confident that all dreams must converge into that common dream which provided a sufficient semblance to reality.

As we attempted to move forward our limbs evaded our control. Arms and legs seemed determined to pursue their own dream so that our bodies jostled against each other as we struggled to move across an island of indefinite substance. For this reason, each of us authored within our minds a survey of a different island, and despite our efforts each of our surveys amounted to nothing more than the elaboration of a fictive conjecture.

Events and their perceptions twined and blended like wisps of colored smoke. Our survey proceeded without motion, an excavations began and concluded at the same instant and with the same gesture. Objects were exposed only to disappear and inscriptions like palindromes read the same from every direction. A stream which seemed to flow wide and slow-moving appeared to others as narrow and agitated; a mountain whose flat and serene face appeared unapproachable was recognized by others as a gentle, green-shrouded hill; trees whose trunks appeared broad as houses were recognized as mere shrubs festooned with large and sweet-smelling violet flowers. Above our heads from various directions and all angles the sun and moon traded places with startling abruptness. We watched each other manipulate shovels whose handles were as thin and twisted as tree-branches, push wheelbarrows that wobbled as awkward as lead pillows, wrestle with buckets the size and shape of tea-cups. And most disturbing, those crates we were certain we methodically filled with samples all emptied themselves, just as our notebooks whose pages we covered with figures and numbers became suddenly blank, as though their marks simply had slipped from the page. Even our microscopes and compasses revealed themselves as constructs made of painted cardboard and delusion.

We had long before this abandoned all thought of food or drink or sleep, since our dreams had reduced us to a pure mentality. That which we were confident had been accomplished disappeared in a tremulous swirl of gray haze. We called to each other in silence, our mouths open and our throats lined with cotton. Each gesture of our bodies became more and other, until movement itself blurred into alternately bright and dark shadow. Our sighs of frustration, confusion and self-doubt became melodic and then multiplied until they became symphonic. If any initiated action reached a conclusion, none of us recognized it or even paused to wonder.

Distinctions between dreams became evaluations of their dreamers. We discovered that certain dreamers populated their dreams with exotic and even disturbing beings. Was that exoticism an element of the dreamer's personality or an inevitable generation of an undisciplined mind loosed from its leash, or worse, a self-conscious invention of its dreamer? But our confusion concerning the exploration of this dreamscape island broadened like a spreading stain until we were compelled to suspect we had migrated into the same dream.

In this dream of darkness, sunshine fell as a sudden and darkly syrupy iridescent mist until every object was sheathed in the gleam of a black pearl. The contours of our dreams became shrouded by this perplexing darkness although the pattern of the dreams remained distinctive. And to our surprise, with this elaboration suddenly we were able to pursue the inhabitant.

His appearance was inscrutable beyond being short of stature and slight of build. Within our dream of darkness his brighter darkness glittered as tarnished silver upon darker gray shrouded within a still deeper blue-blackness. His movements appeared swift, actions of arms and legs mere blurs impossible to follow with the eye and stuttering as in a movie-strip with alternating image frames removed. Having identified him uniquely, we concluded that others surrounded us and that they had done so from the moment of our arrival, albeit invisible within that shared dream of dark sunlight splashing onto glistening green vegetation and fiercely bright yellow sand. This inhabitant and his invisible companions somehow had recognized every blind spot within our vision and then hidden there determined to study us without our knowledge until our dreams became visions within which they could migrate unrecognized and unrecognizable. So when we began to follow the inhabitant he already knew that we would do so, and knew as well how all of this would end.

Our pursuit needed to be made, just as his avoidance and devious misdirections needed to be made. We danced with the inhabitant as one might with a swarm of pale glowing fireflies. Together we followed the inhabitant along vegetation-choked paths that wound around the cluttered base of the volcano and meandered through its swamps populated by metallic snakes and liquid lizards and transparent frogs and we struggled to skirt treacherous ravines by following serpentine routes that led us past speckled tress and confettied shrubs. Eventually the path of the inhabitant moved upward along the flank of the volcano and we were compelled to follow.

Midway to the volcano's summit, a roughly-triangular promontory of solid blue-black rock devoid of vegetation jutted from its side to reach out over the steel-blue beach below. Near that promontory's tip a small fire gave off a flickering light of blue and green and dark orange sparkling in our viscous air. Drawing closer we spied the inhabitant squatting alone beside that fire, his skin scintillating from blue to orange to green illuminated by the fire's shifting light. The inhabitant stared morosely into this fire's heart as if receiving messages or perhaps merely reading signs.

We stood in a semicircle to block the path from the base of this promontory determined that the inhabitant must not be permitted to retreat unobserved. We moved cautiously forward hopeful of interrogating him and perhaps learning about this island and especially about those other inhabitants. As we watched, dreams erupted from the fire as darkly-tinted clouds shaped as large, fog-filled bubbles. The inhabitant scrutinized each of these bubbles, watched each rise and drift, as if awaiting revelation. We suspected that for the inhabitant our dreams possessed colors which he perceived as sounds, and those sounds which we believed we recognized were instead aromas. Each sensation linked to each of those manifestations appeared to be perceived by this inhabitant along a spectrum that suggested differences without distinctions.

Then as we watched, the inhabitant waved his hands over his opaquely shimmering fire as though sorting each of those bubble-clouds. Fascinated, we moved closer until we were convinced we recognized within one bubble the figure of our ship, and within another bubble a man who resembled our Captain as he addressed us in silence. And then within bubble after bubble drifting above that fire we recognized each other as ourselves. We wondered then if in the end it was the inhabitant who conjured each of our layers of translucent dreams to be stacked and examined like geological strata.

Although we did not know whether the inhabitant realized we surrounded him, we assumed he knew of our existence and surmised our general location. But he gave no indication, nor gestured as if attempting to address us. Each of our convictions embodied its own contradiction so that even they seemed traps built with shattered mirrors. Had we all been drunks flailing about within the same stupor we could not have accomplished less or have been more baffled by that failure.

The inhabitant, meanwhile, scrutinized with large and sparkling eyes that freakish fire and its boiling foam of drifting images. We assumed that this distraction allowed us to approach still closer. Moving forward with the infinite slowness of a dream, time ceased to pass while each moment inflated. This moment which we conjectured gradually embraced the inhabitant and then his fire and then the promontory upon which he perched, until finally it had embraced all of us together on this island. And then the inhabitant looked up.

His gleaming faceted turquoise eyes moved from one of us to the next as if challenging each individuation until our separate unities were dissolved. We observed ourselves observing each other as observed by the inhabitant. His awareness had infused our own and we anticipated the resolution of discrepancies and the harmonizing of contradictions. But instead, we were startled to detect musical sounds that were not music, while at the same moment the aroma of ripe apples filled the air around us. We looked about for the source of those sounds and for that aroma while the inhabitant stared at each of us individually as if anticipating some recognition or response on our part. As though the inhabitant had initiated a conversation and now expected we would continue it.

We looked at each other unsure how we might elaborate what the inhabitant appeared to offer, eager to continue this communication and perhaps resolve our questions.

But the inhabitant had discovered something about us, or perhaps had merely recognized something, which we should have known but either had failed to see or refused to acknowledge. To this point we had seen without seeing and we now hoped the certainty of our vision would return. As sounds which were not sounds elaborated within our dreams into a low and throaty roar, that aroma of apples revealed itself to be that of burning wood laced with the smell of burning tar. Simultaneously all of us turned to look out toward the lagoon. Startled and then horrified, we discovered dazzling orange flames and billowing black smoke rising from our ship. Suddenly the question of what was a dream and what was reality evaporated. We turned to the inhabitant as though he understood what we merely observed. And the inhabitant looked back at us as if seeing us for who we really were, beings trapped within a carapace of ignorance and fear. And then perhaps he smiled.

In that iridescent darkness the inhabitant's face became a rippling silver mist without edges or contours, yet a smile, perhaps even a grin, drifted languorously within its fog. The inhabitant's expression suggested a deeper understanding than we were capable of, and it was this revelation of our insufficiency as much as the sight of our ship which triggered a panic among us. Sudden and abject terror scattered us like cockroaches on a kitchen wall. A light resembling illumination had come on and we each fled without plan or thought except self-preservation.

Every intention evaporated from our minds as panic sent us racing heedless of each other's path. We moved somehow without moving and yet soon became breathless with urgency. Casting its shadow over our unique dreams, fear scattered us like dry leaves before an autumn wind. Our selves were frantic to resume our disguises of self as terror rebuilt those barriers which had dissolved within our common quest. Fear now defined us more completely than any aspiration or expectation. And perhaps this was what the inhabitant recognized. Our hopes might bind us, but our fears separated us decisively and thereby completed our individuation.

Meanwhile our ship was ablaze and we were helpless to intervene. As if a closer proximity to the ship would prove useful, we fled down the side of the volcano and raced to the beach even while in our confusion we could only guess its direction. But we fled, or at least we seemed to flee, unless it was our common dream itself which moved. This decision which was not a decision must have been anticipated by the inhabitant. Whether amused by our panic or perhaps embarrassed by it, the inhabitant suddenly stood from the fire, ran toward the point of the promontory and then at its tip and with his thin and naked arms spread from his sides, leaped into open, empty air.

We watched, or at least we believed that we watched, the inhabitant now soar above our heads and then dive down and then soar again as though riding invisible waves. The inhabitant turned in the black sky and wheeled to pass directly over us before swooping low over his abandoned fire. At his passing that fire's tiny flames leaped into the sky as a sudden and enormous geyser of brilliantly fierce light.

This blistering light stopped each of us in our flight and compelled us to look up. The darkness surrounding us remained a black and viscous syrup clinging to whatever it touched and our attempts to wipe it from our eyes left our hands covered and slippery. But even scattered as we were, we watched the inhabitant's flight, watched him swoop and soar before he turned toward the lagoon. Approaching our burning vessel he swooped down and then soared trailing a huge flame that exploded from the ship. Within moments our ship was wrapped in flames and then reduced to a smoldering and smoking hulk of orange-glowing debris.

When finally we all gathered together at the water's edge to watch the destruction of that ship which sustained us, despair overwhelmed us. Sorting through our layers of dreams only to discover the destruction of our ship at the end submerged our exploration of the island within a swamp made up of channels of despair and backwaters of terror surrounding the bottomless pool of failed understanding.

But perhaps in the end it was our Captain within his own dream which nested within our communal dream who had successfully anticipated all of this, because somehow we all discovered ourselves suddenly yet certainly standing together on the deck of our ship and rescued from the island.

Astounded, we looked about to find that our ship remained as we had left it while the sun battered us to wash away every dream. We stared across the lagoon and our island appeared as we recalled seeing it when our ship first dropped anchor. Although we remained uncertain how our rescue had been effected we all agreed that we now stood together at the rail on the deck of our ship looking out toward that island as if we had never visited it.

Acknowledging finally that our survey had failed and our expedition had collapsed into fragments and confusion, our Captain ordered his crew to set sail and we moved on. Our team gathered at the stern to watch in frustration as that island, our destination and the object of our fascination, grew small retreating toward the horizon. As the island receded our frustration increased until we turned to the Captain demanding that he return us to the island. We assured him that our survey could still succeed; that somehow but inevitably we would have adjusted to the island's hostility and illusions and so would have wrested from it every secret and brought its confusion of realities within our realm of certainties.

The Captain listened to us patiently and he was attentive to our ambitions as well as our concerns. Reminding us of those dangers we had only just avoided, he insisted that simply because we had already been there and had avoided them did not inoculate us against other and perhaps far worse dangers. He insisted that we were no better equipped against the island's deceptions than we had been upon first landing. But our geologist replied that just the opposite was the case; that precisely as a result of our visit we knew not only what we needed to avoid, but we had gained a clearer notion of what our objective needed to be. The Captain looked from one to the other of us with pained annoyance but something we said must have changed his mind because he turned to the first-mate and ordered him to sail back to the island. The first-mate appeared tempted to protest, but instead he issued the appropriate orders. Regardless of the wisdom, we were determined to try again to expose this island's secrets.

We sailed until eventually we reached the island's coordinates. Yet we needed to check our charts and then take additional measurements to be certain we had reached its location because the island itself was no longer there.

Since this seemed unlikely, the Captain sailed further on the possibility that our charts and instruments had been misread. But after sailing for several hours around what should have been the island's location we found no evidence that any island had ever existed there. Our confusion left us depressed and we paced the deck silent and sullen. But finally the first-mate stepped forward to provide an explanation.

Although what he said seemed both fantastic and contrived, his explanation covered those facts with which we were familiar.

As the first-mate explained it, the inhabitants of the island had watched us from the instant we dropped anchor in the lagoon, observing not only how we went about our activities but had scrutinized each of us individually, confident they recognized not only who we were and why we were but finally what we were. And by our actions and decisions we had settled each of their unresolved questions. So when we panicked at the thought of being left isolated and alone on their island by the burning of our ship, as though this was some terrible fate which we needed to avoid, this confirmed for the inhabitants all that they needed to know.

While we were prepared to concede all of this, we could not conjecture how that could cause the island to disappear, and especially whether that disappearance had been the result of some inscrutable natural process or some baffling power shared among its inhabitants.

The Captain appeared as confused by the first-mate's account as the rest of us. When questioned, the first-mate looked away saying that all of this was quite simple. Our flight from the island proved that we were not worthy of learning its secrets or discovering more about its inhabitants. By our actions we demonstrated that we had no care for the island beyond what we might gain from it and what we might take away with us, even if that was mere knowledge. We had been granted a glimpse of the inhabitant and yet had failed to recognize what we had seen and then to value that. We had been provided a rare privilege and had wasted that opportunity battling meaningless confusions as well as those puny emotions concerning our selves and their safety. The island's disappearance was their way of informing us that we had wasted the only opportunity any of us would ever have to explore it. He explained that the inhabitants had not moved the island, they had simply made it so thoroughly immaterial that we could sail directly over it and never know that we had done so. He then added that another crew, one that had not yet failed their selves, would need to reach the island before it would once again be accessible to exploration.

We attempted to explain to the first-mate how little sense this all made but he simply shrugged his shoulders and walked away saying that there is a price to every failure and each act of cowardice, and that the only thing to be done with a penalty was to pay it and move on.

And reluctantly, resentfully, that is what we did.

ISLAND OF STONE WOMEN

THE EXPERIENCE AND INSTINCTS OF OUR CAPTAIN and our determination to decipher an incomplete portion of an ancient map have brought us here. It is an island of stones shaped to resemble women formed in lapis lazuli and malachite, porphyry and crystal, jade and agate, marbles of brilliant white, blood red and deathly black, forms of stone streaked and layered in a thousand colors and hues which sparkle in subtle finishes and textures, some as small as pebbles and others approaching the size of mountains. Bodies in every posture and position of work or play, at ease or in conflict, each displays rippling and contoured flesh or clear ridge of bone. Alone, in pairs or small groups, each figure engages in some occupation which is harmonized with or contrasted by the structure and appearance of the stone. Except for the dreamers who abide sleeping, different stones within their caves.

The subject of numerous and startling legends, our island first appears at night like an unrepentant star sparkling on the horizon. It grows brighter each night shimmering in the heavy air until eventually even in daylight it becomes a beacon. Only as we approach the island do its scintillations and the glittering brilliance of its surfaces acquire unexpected precision.

Our ship anchors in a jagged bay just beyond the foaming ridge of breaking waves and as close to shore as we dare before we set out in longboats to land. Our team is determined to explore this island, traverse it in every direction to follow even the faintest and least passable paths. We are determined finally to find the dreamers.

According to one of the legends, recumbent, seated or standing, eyes open or closed, in active observation or pensive reverie watching another light, those dreamers within their caves conjure a separate island, an island of trees resembling men adrift in a sea of a music whose harmonies flow thick as honey around their ears and upon their lips. These trees like men are of every size and species, of rough bark and smooth, of wide soft leaves and short, sharp needles; trees of thick limbs and long flexing boughs and all clothe their island in an embrace of aromatic foliage. Trees that whisper and sigh as they wave in the breeze yearning without hope, and trees that stand firm and confident against the tempest's violence and their own despair. Trees that overhang gurgling crystal streams or perch on the shoulders of sleeping mountains or cluster in thick cool groves within their valleys or most often stand alone in silhouette against our opalescent sky. The dreamers conjure this other island where, when the wind blows the trees all lean together until the sighs of their hopeless desires blend into a tremulous and azure moan.

Night falls and we observe our island of stone women sailing beneath a flat yellow moon. Captured by the dreamers with a thousand strands of silent music, the desires of those trees follow the moon's transit plucking melodically at the light as the moon drifts and swells. Along the edge of the moon, stars like slivers of diamond appear scattered among larger pearls. The sound of continually shattering crystal rises as the moon's silhouette embraces these strands and threads which have woven themselves into that music which also pierces each of us standing on the beach beside our longboat as with a silver needle.

We watch with mouths open as that sound drifts around our feet as a fog just above the sand. And then that light from the moon awakens the dreamers to rise. The dreamers begin to glow, their muted colors becoming deep and vibrant.

Moving beyond the beach we establish our first camp on a ledge at the flank of the volcano, and from there we peer across the bay to that island conjured by the dreamers where those trees hover and sway as a dense and undulating cloud of dark green. Our ship crouches below us trapped within a narrow blue-black channel, all that remains of that inlet by which the island of trees once reached the eastern beach. Our specialist in these matters predicts that the moon will soon reflect its light into the cone of the volcano towering over and behind us. She insists we are fortunate to witness this event; it will justify our having come so far and endured so many dangers.

In that silky moonlight we leave our camp and move further up the side of the volcano in order to better observe this moment. One among us speculates that the resonant harmonies of those frequencies of light which strike the deepest part of the volcanic cone will release a torrent of the tears of those frustrated aspirations of these trees which have been trapped since the birth of the universe. Several among us hypothesize that within deeply buried strata, pure thought has been snared from passing meteors and comets and then frozen within the volcano; those interstellar wanderers profound from long periods of deep thought encapsulate reservoirs of the intergalactic energy which organizes all perception. Such profound inanimates speak with eloquence of their battles and travails, those opportunities embraced or abandoned as the passage of time inscribes itself upon every surface. But graduations in the motion of light blend as the utterly pure expression of inanimate existence; that peculiar condensation of the desires of the inert along with those compressed passions of the motionless. A distillate resembling nectar and comprised of the energy from those actions which remain incomplete or never begun.

The resonant vibrations from this frozen energy projected into the volcano are released suddenly by the shattering power of specific frequencies of the moon's light. Each of these paths provide priceless opportunities for the fundamental research which has opened before us. Or so some among us continue to insist.

Our vigil is long and thrilling, and we return to our camp at sunrise. And to our perplexity we discover signs of disturbance; each commonplace object is found tipped over or moved or set defiantly upside down. Our campsite is subtly but distinctively disturbed. But we find no other sign or mark, neither footprint nor fingerprint to betray a perpetrator. The naked power of thought originating from deep within the volcano is assumed and conversions of potential energy are surmised. In this way we are compelled to recognize a disturbance within our own thinking, a provocative realignment of our strongest and most reliable patterns. By this we recognize ourselves as collaborators in our own terror, a spontaneous and simultaneous abandonment of rational architecture as it shapes our perceptions.

And then, as if provoked by all of this agitation, the dreamers turn.

We know this even before we have returned to the first promontory. The dreamers including those disguised within their caves stir momentarily to awaken and their positions change. One that lay alone now stands sleepily beside two others. Others once clustered together are now separate, outside their group, brooding, isolated and pondering. As if an army of sculptors as numerous and industrious as ants has taken up hammer and chisel re-shaping every stone. Startled we recognize and notate each change, a frenetic gathering of data we can only hope eventually will provide knowledge.

Without regard to its size or material, each shape has been profoundly modified. Some among us propose that a will lurks within the island controlling these changes so that fragments of its intention are inscribed within the profile of each visage. But ambivalence prowls the shadows of every posture; an overwhelming desire to be other and no longer that which is.

Anticipating the return of the moon and its baffling realignments we disperse to search the island obsessed by the conviction that our search will reveal something behind the apparent and hidden beneath the surface. Each of us constructs a gratifying hypothesis, one that resembles that which is known and is demonstrable. As we stumble down or climb up the steep and treacherous sides of the volcano, each of us attempts to fashion a testable assertion. After all, the fabrication of a sustainable hypotheses linking together the elements of those legends is the reason we have made this journey. We are certain such hypotheses will justify our discomfort and confusion and perhaps even redeems our many and baffling failures. Each of our assertions contains its own protocol, its own rationalized collection of a-prior and axiomatic truths along with parameters to confine each variable, and each of them structured within a dimensional dispersion. The members of our team remain busily alert as we anticipate revelation; we suspect it swirls around us like a morning mist though just as hopeless to grasp.

We begin to surmise the location of those hidden dreamers within their caves, their dispersion within space and over time, optimistic this will dispel our confusion by exposing a reassuring pattern. We initiate a catalog and a type-list. We research each observation and list each speculation and by this remain profoundly fascinated. Each dreamer acquires a cult of research. And each of us adopts a notional specialization distinguishable from the research objectives of every other.

Our Captain, meanwhile, has despaired of guiding our ship safely through that narrow channel to reach the island of trees. Strategies are timidly proposed, prognostications of various futures are hypothesized, alternative paths are explicated, debated and homogenized. We struggle to convince him he will overcome this island, until gradually he appears reassured. And then the cook disappears.

It is assumed the cook has gone to the island of trees though for reasons which remain obscure and whose conjectures possess no basis. His departure, abrupt and unexplained, triggers our first sensation of abandonment and despair but also danger. The first mate theorizes alien abduction, while the cabin-boy insists that soon we will all die.

Determined to confine those mysteries confronting him, our Captain attempts again to journey to the island of tress. Unwilling to tolerate our assistance, he travels alone by longboat as if determined to confront his enemy defiantly unarmed. Much of this day passes in ignorant speculation. Upon returning from his unsuccessful attempt at rescue, he tells a remarkable story.

The island of trees, he explains to us, is populated by enormous alligators which never smile. The trees are served by the alligators and communicate to them that music of particular celestial bodies which have accumulated the wisdom of passing comets and shooting stars. Thus, a relationship exists with the dreamers through the music of light. How the posturing dreamers reshape the island of trees and conjure this aggressive population of servile alligators remains inscrutable. Somehow, a moment's possibilities imprint themselves on the contours of the dreams of these dreamers and then reside there for eternity. Creatures ill-formed and devious appear among the crocodiles to feed upon the light, devour each other, and in the next moment drift away as smoke.

Apprised of what our Captain has discovered, alliances and hierarchies dismantle and reassemble in unlikely ways. The operation of perception is debated, the inexplicable must be assumed. Elegance replaces precision, passion displaces rigor. Each hypothesis becomes true, every conjecture a fact, perception itself becomes a method of formulation. Members of our team begin to steal each other's field notes, rewrite each other's reports, falsify the common currency of data elaborated to fill every void, until inscrutable gestures replace speech. And then the team members begin to dream each other.

These renegade dreams conjure various fates which are neither impossible nor inevitable, but drift between extremes of existence like aromatic smoke. We recognize ourselves within those dreams as in a fun-house mirror; distortions recall our resemblances to others and remind us that our futures are not so dissimilar; we each will find that which has always pursued us and this recognition should remind us of our temporality.

Inexplicably, back at the campsite stone facsimiles of our research instruments faithful in the most minute detail begin to appear. This certain evidence of fossilized thought suggests a rigor-mortise in the energy field surrounding us, a backwash of stagnancy and decay within the stream of time. Progression demands sequence and time must pass without error. We acknowledge finally that all can only be true. Uncertain, however, that the Captain has shared all that he has observed, we are tempted to retrace his steps and confront those alligators of truth.

Several of us volunteer to row across the bay to explore the island of trees, but at the beach we discover our boats smashed and useless, their wooden ribs stove-in and pale-bright with their destruction. The culprits responsible remain unknown, but the nature of the damage insists their violence is tremendous and the power behind it more than human and perhaps even other than human. Something is amiss, the formulas do not agree and we speculate that finally we are in danger.

All through the night echoes of an unspecified but exceptional violence shudder the air.

The moon finally approaches a position directly above the cone of the volcano. Its attractive power bends the tip of its crater toward it like a flower pursuing the life-giving sun. Beneath our feet the ground begins to roil and swell, stones become dislodged moving to unlikely and aberrant locations. This motion results in the stone women leaping from their pedestals to occupy those perches and promontories which overlook our camp. Stone women continue to change positions and postures, rearranging themselves within the landscape. Unleashing this activity, the moon gradually comes to hover just above our heads, the peaks of its mountains and the ridges of its craters approach our island. Across the bay the island of trees quavers in the moon-brightened air like a heat mirage, beckoning, seductive, an allure of irresistible power.

The island of trees, meanwhile, has approached us so close that with binoculars we observe those alligators crouching as sentinels beside each tree. Tooth-jeweled jaws spread and rose-quartz throats open releasing a terrible thunder. Leaves on the trees tremble and flash glittering with the nourishment of that sound in the thick wet moonlight.

As if from a huge mirror, the moon-reflected light pierces the darkest recesses of the volcano's cone. And then a frightening sort of thaw begins; whispers and muttering vibrate the air as wisps of blue and violet smoke curl along the edges of the crater. This we recognize as the residue of the sound of thought as it warms and expands and begins to pulse against the crater's crystal walls. Even the crash and boil of the surf becomes drowned out by this sound emanating from the volcano. A chorus of voices begins to rise, its tonality a blend of wish and will which then subsides to be replaced by another chorus of dissonance and doubt. These voices mingle and weave like the fragrances of a forest. Team members bring out note-pads, a mad scramble of transcription begins. Whole phrases like hysterical mosquitoes are snatched from the air by our voracious team. And each phrase yields a subtle vacuum as its words evaporate from beneath our hands so that even their recollection dies in the undulant air.

The manic din of chorus upon chorus rises, harmonies and dissonances cancel out as they jostle against each other in rhythm, until the air begins to shimmer and beat with their excitement. Their confluent blend builds into a wave which rolls over us and also under us. Stones move and then move again. And then the light begins to tremble.

But just as suddenly, all is over. Covered by webs of fine cracks and tiny fissures perhaps the result of those conflicting resonances, and each stone woman begins to shatter. From the largest to the very smallest, veins of rupture appear on their surfaces and then widen. A powerful wind blows down from the cone of the volcano and across the island reducing each stone figure to a pile of pale, shapeless sand. Every boulder, cliff, and pebble shatters into an infinity of tiny shards.

The silent moon begins to ascend, retreating until it is once again small, pale, and inscrutable. As the moon moves away the island of trees descends beneath the sea, swallowed without a murmur or trace, its alligators singing a song of farewell and victorious regret.

We stand together beside our Captain, masters of an island of shifting and billowing sand. We ponder our own regret over those spaces left unfilled while the air takes on the aroma of bitter oranges. Having come so far and accomplished so little, we find ourselves left with our unresolved queries as cold companions abandoned as deeper enigmas, their accumulation the silent demonstration of our own dreams which are now defenseless against their vacuum's undertow.

Our own dreams disappear as the ghosts of thought, their harmonies canceled and then betrayed. Having aspired to embrace our various confusions, we find ourselves swallowed by them. The light of the island has baffled our eyes as its songs have crystallized within our ears. We turn then, searching each other's eyes for the keys to the myriad of mysteries, determined to avoid the temptation to abandon that which remains unresolved. Perplexed by our sense of vacuous betrayal, the surfaces around us defy explication leaving us with perceptions that are both full and empty. The island of trees suggested an explanatory key, and yet, having drifted beyond our observation, that key becomes lost and appears irrecoverable.

Our Captain remains determined and non-pulsed although resentful of having lost his cook yet also unwilling to debate or conjecture pursuit of the island of trees as if even its continued existence has become an annoying speculation.

But it was the volcano after all which brought our mysteries and enigmas to the surface. We console ourselves that it was unlikely we would resolve that which had appeared before us. Some amplify their insistence on a consciousness residing within the volcano, while others dismiss every surmise that leaves unanswered the profound and decisive question of mechanism. We are here, after all, precisely because what is observed remains inexplicable and yet also true. And that which has existed can only have come about by some mechanism inscrutable although real.

Our Captain refrains from every additional conjecture and offers no opinion as to which of our speculations possesses the greatest merit. His concern remains for the cook who has disappeared along with that drifting island of trees.

But in the end we are each compelled to acknowledge that what resists explanation must remain so, at least for the time being. And departure is the only path that retains a justifiable purpose.

We repair the battered boats, our Captain returns us to our ship, and in this way the island is invited to return to its dreams and the conjecture of its lost stone women.

OTHER STORIES

MARTIN AND THE DEAD CATS

THE CAT LAID LENGTHWISE on a gray granite step near the top of the stairway to the Cathedral and in that way that dead cats so often do, legs straight and head hanging off the edge of the step as if hoping to be mistaken for a cat rug. The broad face of the Cathedral and the plaza around it sparkled in a bronze sunrise. Though it interrupted his return to his apartment, Martin climbed to where the large tabby lay. He hoped this cat was merely asleep, but he was alone and a motionless cat made him nervous. He leaned close and although the cat appeared as if it had merely decided to take a nap, Martin assumed otherwise.

Suddenly the empty plaza behind him, along with this dead cat and a certain unsettling quality of the light; all of this was now threatening. Improbable convergences would begin to accumulate, he was confident of that. Since every event has its cause, there had to be a cause to this cat lying on this step in front of this Cathedral. Though that cause had its own cause, and that cause its own cause, in the end there had to be a first cause. Martin wondered if others, perhaps even the Bishop, would insist he was that first cause. His ignorance of those links which led to this cat on this step provided him no protection from the Bishop.

He was tempted to ask if this dead cat belonged to someone inside the Cathedral. But only a year before, the Bishop had turned Martin into a goat, and he was certain the Bishop would take advantage of this mystery to repeat that miserable punishment.

His life as a goat had lasted six months, his punishment for having attempted to seduce the Bishop's niece. Martin had only seen the elderly woman once and had not known who she was. At his trial he had insisted that, although he had found the woman marginally charming, he had behaved respectfully. But power is as power does, and unfortunately for Martin, the fact of his arrest became proof of his guilt. It cost him his job at the Bishop's used car lot along with his apartment and most of his friendships as well as his favorite and most recent girlfriend.

Martin stepped away from the cat and retreated down the Cathedral steps. For the rest of his journey he did not see another human, but he saw three more cats that appeared to be dead. They were different sizes and colors and frozen into unlikely postures at odd locations, but each appeared thoroughly dead. Dead cats lying about unburied, he mused, are best left to be discovered by others.

In the hallway to his apartment Martin stepped to the door of his neighbor and knocked. Arthur, Martin's neighbor, came immediately to the door. His eyes were red. He sobbed, "I can't believe Maxwell is dead."

Martin remembered a slow-moving calico the size of a small dog. He said to Arthur, "Something seems to be up with our cats." Nodding, Arthur invited Martin inside.

Maxwell occupied the center of the coffee table sporting a wide red ribbon tied around its throat in a large bow, a decorative touch that, in life, this cat would never have tolerated. Martin concluded that death leaves us vulnerable to every whim of the living.

Over mugs of hot coffee Arthur said, "Every dead cat is dead, but are any of the causes the same? They must share something beyond the fact that they're cats and they're dead."

Terrifying questions of causality muddled Martin as well. He asked, "You think this has anything to do with the Bishop?" It was widely agreed the Bishop could do whatever he wished, and often did.

Arthur smirked. "You'd like that, wouldn't you."

Before Martin could respond there was a knock on the door. Arthur stood and opened it to usher in a neighbor from further down the hall and mutual friend whose name was April. Her eyes were red. "Carol is dead," she said and then wept in earnest. It took a moment for her to realize that Maxwell was not asleep on the coffee table, and then she cried harder. Arthur embraced her as he led her to the couch. He laid her down and began to unbutton her blouse. Martin stood, placed his coffee cup on the kitchen counter and then walked to the front door. With his hand on the door knob, he noticed that April's jeans had been removed. Bereavement takes many forms, but every loss is an interior scar impossible to assuage. He stepped across the hall to his own apartment.

Inside he saw that the message-light on his answering machine displayed the numeral two. This dead-cat business reminded Martin to suspect all gestures toward communication.

The first message was from his friend Chuck asking to borrow money, and thus was safe for Martin to ignore. He fast-forwarded to the second message.

An officious female voice proclaimed its owner a representative of the Bishop and ordered Martin to appear in the Bishop's office at nine the following morning. The speaker's tone suggested an affirmative reply was assumed inevitable.

There was no escape. Martin had twenty-four hours before he would find himself under the Bishop's thumb. He could only avoid being turned back into a goat, or worse, by solving the mystery of these dead cats himself. So his first impulse was to run away and hide. He packed a bag and left his apartment.

The duty officer at the police station was named Chandler. People had been showing up all morning, he said, eager to put themselves under police protection from the Bishop's office. "This business with the dead cats is a hell of a thing if you ask me." He took Martin's bag and assigned him a cell on the twelfth floor overlooking the park and the pond. "People started coming in last night," Chandler said, "but this morning it's been a madhouse."

"Does anybody know what's causing this?"

Chandler shrugged and then grinned patiently. "If I had a nickel for every guess I've heard today I'd have a lot of nickels." He looked around before leaning close and whispered, "Only thing makes any sense is the Bishop's behind this. And that's all people need to know."

Martin thanked him and turned to leave promising to return before dark.

He was afraid he would be forced to act alone and he did not like that idea, it smelled worse than a dead cat. He walked to a pay-phone behind the public library planning to call a friend he hoped would help but found a dead cat lying behind it. He decided his call was not important and left.

Martin walked to the office of Dr. Tzara, the city's vet. The willowy blond nurse-receptionist wearing a badge asserting her name was June explained that the doctor had just left for his annual diabolical retreat. She said that by now he, along with one of the local dentists and the editor of the city's newspaper, was involved with either Beelzebub or Satan, she couldn't be sure which. She added that with Dr. Tzara gone, she herself had nothing to do for the rest of the day. She began to unbutton her blouse.

Martin asked what she knew of the epidemic of cat-deaths. June said she had no opinion, but it was widely believed the Bishop was involved, and that she herself was glad to be well out of it. Martin said he found this curious since cats were among Dr. Tzara's customers. He then asked if she had any suspects. June said she did, but she'd already signed a contract to sell her story to a tabloid so she really couldn't share. By now, most of June's uniform puddled around her feet. When he mentioned his appointment with the Bishop's office, she expressed alarm and called security. He left before the guard arrived regretting that he would miss watching her dress again.

On his way out, Martin just avoided stepping on a dead cat lying stretched across Dr. Tzara's front step. His confusion deepened. It hadn't been there when he arrived. It lay oddly curled as if hoping to be mistaken for a cat hat. Whoever they were, they must be closing in. He was out of options; he must visit the Zoo. If anyone knew anything, someone there must know more.

Through a crackling intercom the Zoo's director refused to speak to Martin, although he acknowledged the conundrum that he was at that moment speaking to Martin about not speaking to him. It seemed obvious to Martin that this man had been reached. He slipped through a gap in the gate and entered the Zoo proper. As he walked he turned frequently frustrated he could not see whoever it was he knew must be following him. He arrived at the lion-house in time for the animals' feeding. When the keeper appeared he called her aside. The lions became restless with her withdrawal of attention but otherwise appeared healthy.

The name printed on the keeper's identity tag was May, though Martin remained skeptical. She was a middle-aged, tall and slim and good-looking, and he decided he would make love to her if that proved useful to his investigation. Between cages that smelled of chlorine Martin asked, "How are your lions?"

"Fine," May said smiling curiously. Somewhat taller than Martin, she seemed unlikely to take off her clothes just then, though he cultivated a hope. "Don't you agree?"

"Appearances are deceiving." He stepped closer, looked directly into her eyes. "There are many dead cats. As you've heard, cats are becoming dead everywhere."

She eyed Martin thoughtfully. "Cats do that from time to time," she said, "although it's unlikely any individual cat will do that more than once."

"These cats lay about losing their organic organization," Martin announced with frightened exasperation. "Overcome in mid-stride and deflated like punctured balloons. Yet there seems no unifying agent. Doesn't this strike you as odd?"

He appeared finally to have captured May's attention. After a moment's hesitation she glanced at her restless lions. "Lions are members of the cat family," she said without conviction. "One assumes they're vulnerable to the cat-death you so graphically describe, yet these appear unaffected."

Annoyed, Martin could not contradict this observation. "And have you visited your tigers today?"

May's eyes widened; she turned and began to run. Martin followed, confident of her destination.

He caught up to her standing beside the tiger cage. One of the tigers roared when Martin appeared and then charged the fence. It appeared quite healthy, yet May's expression was darkly serious. He asked, "Care to visit the cage of cheetahs?"

"We'll only find them apparently healthy as well," May said. She turned abruptly toward Martin. "This is a complex problem. It appears that only house cats are dying; cats living in the company of people." May quietly added, "Dying for the love of humans."

"But that seems so unlikely," Martin said, less certain than he wanted to be.

May suddenly appeared depressed. "Maybe it's a disease humans are giving the cats."

Martin shook his head. "Your cats eat enough people to catch any human diseases going around." He wasn't certain about this, but it seemed reasonable. "Besides, wouldn't humans be getting sick as well?"

May's expression became skeptical. "It doesn't usually work that way."

But Martin had begun to wonder. "It would explain why you don't see many people walking around. It's a perfectly nice day, but we're the only two here."

"Maybe people are at home mourning their demised cats," May suggested. Then she glanced into Martin's eyes. "Or hiding from the Bishop."

Martin looked down and then shrugged. "I should go, but thanks for the advice."

"What will you do?" May asked, and he thought he heard earnest concern in her voice. "You can't just go out there alone, not knowing."

"If I don't solve this myself, the Bishop will blame it on me. When he announces that I'm causing cats to die, I'll be torn to pieces. Cat people are like that, you know."

"No one could believe you're responsible."

"People with dead cats in their arms will believe anything the Bishop tells them." Martin was certain of this. He turned and took two steps before May called him back.

From the breast pocket of her uniform she brought out a piece of paper and a pencil stub. Leaning against the low stone wall she wrote and then handed the paper to Martin. "Make sure when you call this number it's from a pay phone and miles from here." She smiled and then kissed him on the cheek. "For a cat-killer you're not so bad. Look me up when this is over."

May's good wishes cheered Martin and he put them in his pocket beside her note.

At the gates of the Zoo he caught a cross-town bus and half an hour later got off at the far-edge of the city. He found a phone booth and brought out May's note. As he did this the enclosed phone booth filled with a remarkable aroma; something sharp and spicy different from the heavier scent of human urine surrounding him. He brought her note to his nose and discovered the fragrance was emanating from its paper. He was startled by his own excitement. His hand trembled as he keyed in the numbers written on the paper.

The thick and deep voice of an older man answered, "Hello?"

Martin explained that he needed answers to certain question involving cats. After a moment's silence the deep voice gave him an address and time to meet before the line went dead.

He sniffed again at the piece of paper as he hung up the phone. He was tempted to return to the Zoo and to May, but the voice on the telephone had given him little time. Besides, by now May might have reported their conversation to the Bishop.

Though he had noticed none on his first trip, he counted thirteen dead cats visible from the bus as he journeyed back into the city. Some appeared as cat-gloves, others resembled cat-slippers or cat-elbow patches or cat-bras and cat-panties and even cat-thongs. None of this made sense to him, but he concluded finally that it did not matter. But when he arrived at his rendezvous, he knew everything had gone wrong.

The bus pulled away leaving Martin to discover that the address he had been given was a weed-filled lot. He walked further to be certain, so it took some moments to decide he had better flee. But too late; a shiny, black car pulled up to the curb beside him. The two dark-suited men who emerged were grimly silent as they grabbed Martin's arms and hustled him inside. Resistance appeared pointless and he resigned himself to one more future beyond his control.

The windows of the car were black and Martin did not see where they were going. But their ride was brief and when they stopped and the door opened he guessed they were at the back of an underground parking garage. The men pushed him to a narrow elevator. He had a chance to study his captors but decided this was without purpose since he would never see them again.

When the elevator doors opened Martin was led along a featureless concrete hallway ending at an unmarked metal door painted flat gray. One of the men unlocked it and they entered a broad, tall-windowed room. The last of the day's sunlight slanted through a fog of glittering dust that filled the air revealing a world of books and their many shelves. Every size, thickness and binding, piled, stacked or lying open, books occupied every available flat space. Shelves reaching to the dimly distant ceiling sagged and bowed under the weight of even more.

The Old Man was tall, bearded and bearish and he stood at the center of this agglutination of books. His face was lined from the sun, unevenly shaved and bloated with drink, his wiry gray hair was less combed than moved around and long black and gray hairs curled arrogantly from each of his ears. But his expression struck Martin as profound. Before him stood a lectern wide enough to support several books opened at once. The piles of rotting paper filling the room exuded the acrid aroma of our abandoned and decaying past.

The Old Man said nothing but peered anxiously between three open texts with a confounded perplexity. Yet Martin guessed that this man braided within his mind grand and deep thoughts into a single rope of wisdom. The Old Man coughed and then spoke.

"Chaology is the theological study of that which existed before the Creation. Because chaos is not random. A truly random world is one in which an effect can precede its cause. This world came out of Chaos, not out of the Arbitrary. Causality therefore pre-dates the moment of Creation. It exists because it was caused, and causality, though chaotic, is not random." Martin said nothing, simply relieved that this man was not the Bishop.

The Old Man looked up, seemed to consider something, and then returned his attention to the books open before him. "Every logic assumes that first there is a cause which is then followed by its effect. There is no logic in any metaphysic whose first premise is that the effect precedes its cause. Analysis begins with the conviction that every state of affairs has been preceded by a different but commensurable state of affairs within which lays its cause. Only in this way is it possible through a retrograde of deduction to establish an initial cause. This is an absolute law which controls until we reach the quantum level. There, all notions of cause and effect break down. As the physicists say, at the quantum level it's all about dice."

Martin said, "So you've figured out the cat-deaths. Is that what this is about?"

"But, as everyone knows," the Old Man continued as if Martin had not spoken, "this is a probabilistic Universe, and so every logic yields only a probability prediction of a cause. The measure of the probability of any reality lies between zero, which is the Impossible, and one, which is the Inevitable. Every possibility, no matter how close to zero, has a chance of coming into existence, even at the quantum level and for micro-seconds of duration."

"Did you read that," Martin asked, "or did you think it all up yourself?"

The Old Man turned and looked at him. He had small sad eyes which did not suggest sympathy. "But now we have you pursued by the Bishop, who is not a stupid man. We also have variously dead cats. As you well know, the Bishop is an unimaginative man who does not enjoy puzzles. He is, however, not devoid of subtleties. It demands less imagination than patience to sketch a probability curve in which the deaths of these cats is an effect of which you are the cause. So let me ask you; could any of this be karmic?"

The Old Man's question baffled Martin. "I beg your pardon?"

"Karma; that cosmic credit card which can be overdrawn. I'm asking if this could be about your being a really bad guy; somebody who does atrocious things to infants and small animals."

"No! Absolutely not!" The question left Martin furious and horrified. "Why would I do such a thing?"

"Fair enough," the Old Man said and shrugged. "But maybe you were a really bad person in some previous existence. Maybe you were so bad that your karma was ruined for a thousand years." When Martin said nothing, the Old Man nodded. "Yeah, I'm with you. I don't like that idea either, mostly because it assumes we've been here before, and that possibility just pisses me off." Digging into his left ear with his small finger he said, "Well, maybe you're a really bad guy some other way. Ever deal in other people's money?"

This question also horrified Martin. "No; why?" Suddenly he was relieved he had decided not to lend money to Chuck.

"Then at least there's a chance this has nothing to do with your karma."

"So, is this where you decide my situation is hopeless?"

The Old Man sighed and a contemplative veil fell over his eyes. "Not just yet," he said. "I'm saving that for later. Your only hope rests in the impossible occasion of an effect preceding its cause. After all, it's significant that these cats are determined in their final moments of consciousness to appear as articles of human clothing; as if convinced even in death to remain close to their owners because they expect to return. Makes you think, or at least it ought to. But you should be relieved that this improbable hypothesis provides the testable prediction that within a few days, all of these dead cats will return to life"

"Oh good," Martin said sarcastically. "I'm saved."

"Sorry but it isn't that easy. According to these books, at first all of the dead cats will revive though appear ill until gradually they become healthy. In short, within a brief period of time each will resume that state of health it possessed at the moment of its apparent death."

Martin could not disguise his despair but said nothing.

The Old Man straightened. "Granted, there's little chance this speculation will prove useful to your situation. But at least I offer the assurance you will not die for the wrong reason. That's something more than nothing."

"Will thank-you suffice," Martin asked without meeting the Old Man's eyes, "or should I write a check?"

"Cash is always nice," the Old Man said with a smile resembling a grimace. "In any case, my speculation will be useless to you if the Bishop carries out your sentence before these cats return to life. Your predicament is such that if the Bishop convicts you before the cats return to life, and then they do, he will claim it is proof of your guilt, of his justice and of God's love."

Martin was too discouraged to speak and the Old Man appeared to recognize this. "Perhaps all of this is a plot by the Bishop to exact a revenge on you."

"But what could I have done to deserve it?"

"Punishment for the arrogance of having been his thoroughly submissive and penitential victim. After all, you never gave him what he wanted most; something to justify the extension of your enslavement unto eternity."

Annoyed, Martin said, "He added weeks to my goat-life anyway."

"But only after your submission was so complete that your gravest punishment could only be your release. In that way you forced him to change you back into a human being. He'll never forgive you for that."

Martin sighed. "This doesn't seem fair."

"Of course it isn't fair. Fairness implies justice. But in a world where an effect sometimes precedes its cause, justice is accidental and injustice inevitable."

"And yet," Martin said, "you allow a ray of hope."

The Old Man chuckled and turned each of the topmost pages to the three texts open before him. "Don't play the fool. Whatever happens is inevitable, even the impossible. So let me put forward what I believe is your best chance of avoiding the Bishop's wrath. In a multiverse of parallel universes, a universe must exist where you can't be accused of causing these cats to die. Of course, we don't know whether there are a billion such universes or only one, but there must be at least one. This being mathematically true, I simply need to find that universe and then get you there." He grinned at Martin. "Problem solved!"

Martin shook his head. "You're even more nuts than the Bishop. People don't move between universes."

"I didn't say it was simple. Keep in mind that impervious materiality is reality's best disguise. But from what these books suggest, at the quantum scale it is impossible to distinguish any specific universe since all exist simultaneously. Thus, at that scale it should be possible to pass your atomic particles into another universe. At least that's what it says here." The Old Man looked up and directly into Martin's eyes. "Ready to go?"

Later that night and after hours of unsuccessful effort, Martin fled determined to reach his sanctuary with Officer Chandler at the police station. He still held out hope of returning to the Zoo and finding affectionate indifference in the arms of May. The Bishop's men captured him within minutes.

With remarkable speed uncomplicated by deliberation, the Bishop's hand-picked conclave found Martin guilty of causing the deaths of those cats which were dead. The Bishop attempted to convict him of the deaths of those cats still alive, but oddly enough he failed. Martin's existence as a human being was demonstrated to be the sufficient although not the necessary cause of these cat-deaths, but it was enough. He was sentenced to life imprisonment as a bear.

His attorney pleaded for a dignified sentence for Martin, perhaps as a Kodiak Brown Bear, or even a Grizzly Bear. But the Bishop decided he should live out his years behind bars at the city's Zoo as one of those South American bears at which people wantonly throw unlikely objects. Martin's sentence was executed immediately; he entered the Bishop's Chambers a man on two feet, and two hours later was led out by a heavy chain on all four. Upon hearing the Bishop's decision, May swore she would visit Martin every day. He took some comfort from this, but soon discovered that not every promise is a prediction.

Meanwhile, within forty-eight hours of Martin's conviction, the dead cats began to return to life. Everyone except Martin was relieved. And as the Old Man predicted, the Bishop insisted that this proved he was responsible for these deplorable cat-deaths, and therefore the Bishop was still loved by God. In this way the Old Man revived Martin's uncertain faith in prediction.

When the old Bishop eventually died a new Bishop was appointed his replacement. As a gesture of reconciliation, this new Bishop offered Martin a suspension of his sentence and a chance to return to his two-legged form with its quotidian life of freedom within limits, but only if he promised never again to cause the deaths of cats. The little bear that he had become complained loudly, threw itself against its cage and bit several attendants. The new Bishop eventually abandoned his case and, instead, restored a hamster named Metcalfe to his full stature as a tax lawyer. He had become subject to punishment when he was discovered laundering drug-cash through the bank accounts of several of the old Bishop's favorite charities without sharing the proceeds with the Bishop. Restored to his previous state, the new Bishop wished Mr. Metcalfe good fortune on this freshly-reformed life and offered him a job with the Diocese.

Although his thoughts sometimes drifted back to his brief encounter with the charming May, Martin became comfortable in his life as a bear, confident that at least he would never again be accused of causing cats to die, and so never again would be changed into anything else. But every prediction is not a promise.

I SHOT JFK, TOO!

I WAS VERY YOUNG then as were we all. It was fall and the taste of frost spiced every morning with the tart sweetness of a bright red apple. And despite the squalid idiocy of its declaration, I was utterly in love.

Now I insist to myself it was simply because she was so terribly beautiful that I shot him. He was also quite beautiful, of course, but that fact simply complicated my feelings. Perhaps my true intention had always been to shred his tapestry of undeserved grace, to tatter his animal charm and perverse elegance, qualities more appropriate to the movie screen than to an office of public trust. So, unlike the self-aggrandizement of all those hovering around him, mine was a crime of romantic aesthetics. But this irony will never redeem itself.

At that time, however, I knew only that I must free this angelic being from his perverted and despicable clutches. Since that time I have come to realize that my crime was an attempt to re-ignite an inevitably guttering passion. Desperate over our lost love, I convinced myself that his demise would finally bind her to me. What I had not recognized was how that crime would bind all three of us together and forever. I believed that the blood I was determined to shed would nurture the new life of our total love. Although there were many pleasures in that final bloody act, I never guessed that under that hail of bullets, it was our pure and urgent love that would die.

The long journey to his murder was complicated, as is only appropriate for a love such as ours, and its final destination was not apparent, at least not at the beginning. Because from the beginning I assumed that the use of firearms would only pollute his sacrifice and make our devotion unworthy. My mind came alive with schemes to terminate his existence that were each more subtle and more audacious, and certainly more creative, than a gritty and prosaic gun.

As a result, in the fever of my insistence that mine must be a plan of startling originality to be worthy of her, for my first attempt at his termination I decided to divert his Presidential Motorcade off a cliff. In dreams I watched those shinny black limousines hurtle and plummet from the edge of the cliff, awkward and tumbling like helpless black turtles until each crashed to the valley floor in a thunder of crunching metal and shattering glass, followed by the desert's profound silence and a drifting cloud of yellow dust.

Certain there was no way my plan could fail, from the Acme Signage Company I purchased six large and deceptive directional signs made up like enormous arrows that blinked in primary colors. These signs announced the presence of valuable free prizes just ahead. They were, I recognize now, really terrific signs and I was fortunate to have them.

Though I remain convinced this plan was flawless, to my astonishment the motorcade's drivers ignored that forest of enticing arrows. Paralyzed with despair I watched their unbroken line of red tail lights diminish and then blink out at the horizon. I was devastated. In disheartened resignation and tormented by the dimension of my failure, I staggered along the display I had created trying to discover its flaw. And that is how I stumbled from that precarious precipice. The irony is not lost on me that it was I who was the first to fall, and not him. True love is always so heartless.

My prize for this bungled attempt was a stay of several weeks in the hospital suspended in traction, followed by more weeks of physical therapy. But my recovery turned out to be time very well-spent, for by the time I was released I had conceived a new strategy both more subtle and more brazen.

Through a catalog from Acme Land Mines I purchased several kits of said product, and with them laid an elaborate, and what I remain certain was baffling, trap. Yet a glance at the newspaper of the day will reveal that the Presidential Motorcade passed right over my powerful and devious trap without so much as a hiccup, and then drove uneventfully on. When his motorcade finally passed out of sight, once again I could not resist the temptation to see what had gone wrong. It was in this way that I became myself blown up. I remember with unnerving clarity that oddly vertiginous flight as I sailed high into the air leaving a trail of billowing black smoke, my body charred and shriveled from the heat of the blast. Once again I was the unique audience for my ingenious performance and thus the victim of my own device. I should have learned something that day, yet I remain unsure what that could have been.

My recuperation in the hospital was once again lengthy, but also once again I made sure that time was well-spent. For my next attempt I borrowed a plan I knew had worked for one of my more successful colleagues, and so I proceeded certain it would yield the result I desired.

Released from the hospital I contacted the Acme Piano Company. From them I hired four burly but friendly men to suspend one of their pianos from the edge of a cliff with its rope connected to a trip-wire attached to the roadway below. Swaying black and glittering in the sunshine so high above the valley floor, I could only find the sight of that piano majestic and nearly profound But once again, and to my complete surprise, those crafty devils of the Secret Service managed to lead the Presidential Motorcade right over that wire without the slightest hint of incident.

With wild and embarrassing gestures accompanied by my loud cries for help, I tried to lure the motorcade back. Unfortunately, in this way I succeeded in tripping the wire myself. Suspended so high up, the piano fell upon me with such tremendous force that my body was driven like a tent-peg into the very hard and stony ground. I derived no pleasure from that experience but I recognized it as a considerable improvement over being blown-up.

Once again my long recuperation in the hospital provided a pain-filled but effective incubator for one more plan. Someday I hope to write personal notes of thanks to all of the many patient and knowledgeable medical staff who attended me so thoughtfully and so often. By their efforts I remained to fight again.

This time, upon my release I contacted the Acme Rocket Company, and from a very knowledgeable salesman purchased a really large rocket. It is always a pleasure to deal with professionals; I only needed to explain to this man my problem once, and instantly he recognized a solution. He made certain the factory that manufactured the rocket included a harness with which I could strap myself directly to its side. Clutching the ignition switch in my sweaty and nervous hand I waited as the Presidential Motorcade approached. Quickly I calculated wind direction and velocity and made the appropriate adjustments. My hopes were high which merely assured my disappointment. When I pressed the switch, this very expensive rocket veered wildly. I overshot the President's limousine, became buried to my spindly ankles in the canyon wall beyond and then I was blown up. This proved far more painful than I could have anticipated. My body was reduced to large and irregular chunks of stew meat which demanded considerable time and skill to reassemble.

Meanwhile, those of my friends still intrigued by my romantic quest warned me that she was incapable of returning my love. They insisted she held herself above me; regarded me as merely a clown suitable only for the momentary distraction of not very clever children, a cartoon character of the lowest order.

But here's the funny thing about love; under its spell we are each inclined to believe the least likely possibility and to do the craziest things because of it. Empowered now by hindsight, I confess that after these painful reversals, perversely I had come to love him almost as much as I loved her. And perhaps this alone was sufficient justification for his murder. Because my love for her was an ocean, and a life without her love seemed as barren as the surface of the moon. So I concluded it was his presence that withered my edenic garden into a featureless wasteland. Unfortunately, it would demand several more catastrophes before I recognized her as the faithless money-chaser my friends had warned me about.

Painfully and to my eternal embarrassment, I came to treasure her love beyond its true worth. And this, I have recognized, was my deepest mistake. But at the time I believed that when he was dead, if I had engineered that status with some subtlety and style she would recognize my talent and perhaps eventually love me, at least a little. But those were crazy times with a surplus of crazy ideas, as many still remember well.

My trips to the hospital had become so predictable that a particular room was made continually available. And once again, a term reclining in a hospital bed provided the delivery-room for another devious scheme. I was relieved to discover that I had not yet exhausted my arsenal of ideas. Upon my release I contacted the Acme Jet Plane Company and from them purchased the fastest jet they made. My plan had taken on the fiendish yet delusional cleverness of desperation.

Since the results of previous attempts forced me to recognize that my own destruction was likely inevitable, I decided to sacrifice myself and crash directly into the President's limousine. Finally I'd begun to suspect that the relationship she and I shared was in the end impossible. So I came to wonder if without her love there was any point to life. With doubt gnawing at my heart I concluded that she and I would never be together, so if I did not survive, where was my loss?

Strapped into the cockpit of my newest acquisition and flying high over the Presidential motorcade, when I had his limousine in my sights I gunned the engine and pushed the controls to dive. The throttle worked as advertised, the directional controls did not. To my disappointment I traveled all the way around the world, and fourteen hours later crashed into the spot the Presidential limousine had already passed. Unlike my previous attempts, this was worse than embarrassing, it was in fact humiliating. How could such a carefully-laid plan have failed so thoroughly? In a moment of misguided suspicion, I considered no longer purchasing products from the Acme Company. But it is a poor craftsman who blames his tools, or their supplier.

The resulting long recuperation in the hospital from this misadventure gave me ample time to reflect upon each of my previous strategies until I teased out their flaws. Based on this analysis I conceived a new plan, even more dastardly if also more difficult and even more unlikely.

From a cooperative salesman at the Acme Fish Company I purchased a truck-load of live piranha and at a very reasonable price. This done, I then called Marilyn. Fortunately she had not yet left her hotel room, and as difficult as our discussion was, I finally convinced her to break off her date with him. Deeply disappointed and furiously annoyed, she agreed to my request as a personal, show-business favor and I was relieved. I could not tolerate her death on my conscience as well.

That night and under the cover of darkness I dumped that load of piranha into the Presidential Swimming Pool. From behind a line of shrubbery I then watched him some minutes later step out of his dressing robe and dive in. He was such an agile, athletic guy and he swam so beautifully, you could tell he was one of those people who grew up around swimming pools and other people who swam beautifully. But his remarkable athletic prowess earned my deathless respect when I watched him swim past all of those piranha, and then leap balleticaly out of the other end of the pool. Vicious and determined fiends that those piranha are, they leaped out of the water with their tiny, sharp teeth flashing and snapping to follow him. Although the fact of it baffles me to this day, somehow those fish managed to sail over his head and land on me.

In seconds, bits of my skin and flesh hung from my bones like old rags. Some levels of embarrassment are impossible to convey, they must simply be endured in abject silence.

I needed numerous operations by several talented surgeons to become sewn back together, and this was followed by an even longer period of recuperation. So I didn't leave the hospital until nearly his birthday. When finally I was discharged it seemed to me I had reached my lowest ebb. But from a thoroughly-disreputable colleague I stumbled onto what I instantly recognized was the perfect plot for the final—albeit bloody—episode to this joust. For, in addition to my target, my chosen method of execution would likely injure or perhaps even kill the object of my passion. In my own feeble defense I can only say that at this point I could no longer distinguish my love for the one from my desire for the other. Somehow their two beings had become fused, and my enchantment struggled to mutate and adapt to this transformation.

In preparation for our desperate final act I contacted the Acme Bomb Company, and there purchased a small yet powerful bomb. With brilliant cunning I placed it inside his birthday cake and rigged it to go off when it made contact with a metal knife. Though it made me very sad to realize, I was resigned to the fact that many wonderful people would be hurt that night. Not only our adorable Marilyn, there was also Sinatra and Giancana and any number of sturdy underworld celebrities. But believe me; had it been possible I would have placed myself between my love and that explosive confection. At least then I would have been certain that this ridiculous dance of death had ended. I would finally have freed myself from the tyranny of this love, unrequited and unacknowledged, though my liberation would cost my life and the lives of others as well.

From a reporter friend I managed to get a press-pass to his birthday party. When the time came for him to cut the cake I took up a position behind the tv camera crew where I was able to watch on a television monitor the bloody conclusion to these festivities. And because of this I remember all of what followed as an oddly black-and-white dream; that glinting knife coming down, the sudden and uncharacteristic twinge of back pain from his war injury, followed by the knife slipping. Its bright metal edge just caught a corner of the bomb and flipped it high into the air. I lost sight of the bomb on the tv monitor and at first I did not look up. But when finally I did, by some comically unlikely set of circumstances the bomb had already landed in my outstretched hands. The subsequent explosion charred twenty journalists and camera jockeys. I had to be flown to Switzerland to find someone clever enough to wire what was left of me back together.

So yes, of course I shot him. I was there shoulder-to-shoulder with all the others, and we all shot him and for as many different reasons as there were bullets. The CIA and the Mafia and the KGB and Oswald and fundamentalists of differing manias, and of course me. We all shot at him, all at the same time. He occupied the center of a cross-fire even Superman could not have escaped. Of course they grabbed Lee Harvey in the end, but dim-wits create their own bad luck. He was a figure of perpetual gloom, a grim reaper for a world already dead, so only bad things could have happened because of him. His demise was as inevitable as that other's, so by some unlikely logic they deserved each other.

It is impossible to describe the relief I felt in those days immediately after his death. But assuaged by that relief I did not follow subsequent events closely. Simple respect demanded that I wait until after his funeral, invisible and silent, for one full year before I tried to phone her.

To my startled anguish, at first she refused even to speak with me. When finally I bullied my way past the switchboard, she startled me by insisting we had never met, although she admitted she had seen examples of my work on tv. She assured me she had great respect for my art and that she had always been sensitive to the temperaments of visual artists, including those of us engaged in the field of animation. But she refused to concede that she and I had ever enjoyed a relationship. She refused to recall how doggedly I had struggled, and that I, her sworn champion, had made possible her new-found freedom. She would not believe that those many times I risked my life had all been for the sake of her love. She insisted that as far as she was concerned, not even the thinnest of threads bound our two lives together. Unfortunately, in my despair my declarations of ardor quickly became too vehement. I'm certain I raised my voice, and just as certainly I said things I'll forever regret though I fail to remember them at this precise moment. Yet I only recognized how futile my feelings for her were when she told me about that rich Greek boat driver who loaned money to God.

Could this final blow have been any more devastating? Could that fabric of lies I'd woven have been pulled more completely from my eyes to reveal the vacuity of my judgment of her? And worst of all, could my purer love for him have become so thoroughly infected, so utterly diseased, by its shoddy and sordid imitation, that tramp's nightly affection?

Still and despite everything, it gives me no relief that the world remains convinced Oswald did the deed and all by himself. Because really, there was so much lead flying in his direction that day the EPA could have declared an air-pollution alert. In fact, I still find myself amazed that hardly anyone else was hurt. Every gun fired simultaneously, a choreography hardly conceivable unless aided by the most acid of hatred. But people still need to believe it was poor, idiotic Lee Harvey. So if nothing else, I am here to set that record straight. I am tired of other people getting credit for my painful yet superlative efforts. I sacrificed everything, tried every scheme, suffered months of agonizing recuperations, but yet I persisted. Until finally I got him. Though events have proved how wrong-headed I was about her heart, there has been nothing in my life that I have treasured more.

The years have gone by and they have not been unkind. In cold and damp weather all the old wounds cry out, but here in the desert I'm generally quite comfortable. From time to time I still do some cartoon work, pick up a few bucks and keep my hand in. Recently my residuals have become so strong I could probably stop altogether and never have to work again. I've considered moving to Santa Barbara and I've even given some thought to buying a houseboat. But like so much of my otherwise wasted life, my first thought is to recognize that it might have been our boat, it could have been our Santa Barbara.

At the auction conducted after she passed away, I was able to purchase that broach she wore the night of our last dinner together. Once again he had been out somewhere grinning and swaggering on the campaign trail, although by then it had begun to look as if he would likely win. But that night she did not talk about him. She talked only about us. She spoke so softly I needed to lean close to her lips, and her laughter so glittered it left crystal shards under my skin that gradually forced their way into my heart. So now, my only question remains; has anyone ever been so thoroughly and completely in love?

And to those who have, I can only say; you have my sincerest sympathy.

ED DREAMS OF PARIS AND SHOES

STRICTLY SPEAKING, Ed Rodney was an unwilling dreamer except about his '78 Dodge Charger.

In this his favorite dream, Ed pilots the Charger along an empty highway under a sparkling sky. The windows are down, the wind smells of damp earth and wild-flowers, and the engine purrs simply at the pleasure of his presence. This dream fills Ed with a joy that scintillates across his skin and tugs at his scalp, filling him with something he can almost taste. His dream only demands a re-built engine and four good tires, and this Charger restored to life floats at the edge of his mind bright as a fairy's castle.

But, as with most dreams delayed, without that re-built engine the Charger evolved into a turquoise and white hulk. Propped on gray cinder-blocks, brooding wheel-less as if neutered and sheltered beneath a forest-green tarp it crouched all but abandoned behind Ed's mother's garage. He was annoyed to admit that eventually he'd be forced to sell this dream cheap and to any guy who had wheels and an engine, and so he would never drive this Charger even fifty feet. But he would realize none of this until he'd had his dreams about Paris and shoes.

The evening the Charger was first towed behind Ed's mother's garage, the promise of replacing its engine was something close to a vow, his intention as sincere as a religious conviction. But the first weekend after its arrival it rained.

The second weekend it also rained. The third weekend there was a softball game. In fact, Ed had never considered his own inclination to procrastinate, so the temptation to fail his vow amounted to a descent into heresy. After three months his sublime dream had dimmed to an ember, overwhelmed by that corrosive pea-soup fog of mundane existence and quotidian responsibilities.

Fortunately for her, Ed's mother forgot almost instantly that there was a car festering behind her garage. Within hours after the tow-truck drove away, she was no longer upset that a car behind her garage without wheels on cinder-blocks had begun to rot with its hood removed to reveal grease-black parts. She did not even retain the memory of the idea of this mechanical existence. Ed sometimes wondered if she dreamed for them both.

So he could only be startled when, arriving home from work one evening, his mother met him at the front door saying, "It's about that car."

In response to his wide-eyed confusion she added, "A policeman." She appeared to be as surprised as he was. "He wants to talk to you."

A large, thick-necked man wearing a dark uniform stepped up behind her. In a solemn voice he said, "Neighborhood kids got inside that wreck you've got out back. I caught'em smoking a joint." Ed's mother had already disappeared into the shadows of the house trailing a cloud of bafflement and relief.

Ed protested. "The car was all locked up. How'd they get in?"

Big shoulders rose and fell. "Probably shoved something past the window and jammed open the lock."

"So who the hell's going to pay for all that? You police are supposed to protect the property owner. I pay taxes. What are you doing about my property?"

The officer informed Ed Rodney that his property was now officially a public nuisance and he needed to figure out a clever way to move a car without wheels or be ready to pay a lot of money. He then wished Ed a good evening and left. Aflame with righteous outrage as he climbed into his bed, Ed wrestled with the problem of how to move the immovable. It was while pondering this conundrum that Ed endured his first dream of Paris.

Ed sits in an over-stuffed chair in the lobby of the Grand Hotel des Balcones somewhere on the Left Bank of Paris and near the Sorbonne. The windows of the lobby open to a narrow, cobbled street. At Ed's feet, a shaft of thick, late-afternoon sun lays a slab of honey on the black and white marble floor. He smiles recalling that he awaits the arrival of his beautiful wife. Soon he watches her lightly descend the stairs from their room. Each of her steps fills him with a delicious reverence. At the sight of him, his wife smiles. He stands from his chair and she takes his arm. Gracefully as dancers they step out together into a Parisian evening. Nearly every night for a week this dream is repeated for Ed, evolving and elaborating.

Ed's dreams of Paris surprised him and left him befuddled and irritated. Paris was a place he had never even wondered about. Aside from what he had seen of it in movies, the only thing he knew of Paris was that it was the capital of France. He never studied its pictures, didn't know its famous street names or its famous places, knew zero French language. So he was baffled by the reason this dream repeatedly returned him to a place he cared nothing about.

After dinner a week after Ed's visit from the police there was a knock at his mother's front door. Ed opened it to discover a taller boy with reddish hair and looking nearly fifteen, and beside him a smaller, dark-haired boy who might have been thirteen. Quietly the taller one announced, "We need to get into your car."

Ed studied the boys with brightening eyes. "What I got to let you into my car which you already busted into once and got me in trouble and now I got to sell that thing which'll cost me money, and getting the lock fixed already cost me, and now you expect me to just let you into the car. Do I got that all right?"

The taller one said, "We left something."

"No kidding," Ed said caught between fury and surprise. "And the police didn't find it?"

The taller boy shrugged. "They won't find what they don't look for."

The smaller boy added, "Cops aren't all that smart."

"Not smart like you," Ed said.

The smaller one said, "Not even as smart as you."

Ed smirked. The smaller the kid, the bigger the mouth. He debated closing the door on these delinquents when the memory of a new dream from the night before obliterated everything.

Under a Paris evening and with his beautiful wife on his arm, Ed walks along the narrow Rue Casimir Delavigne to the plaza half circling the columned Theatre de l'Odeon, and then beyond it to enter the Luxembourg Garden. Within the Garden they stroll along a sanded path. At the circular reflecting pool they walk past the green and silent queens of France, past the dark green metal chairs ranked as unevenly as bad teeth, past strangers whose glances follow them enchanted by the sight of their happiness. Ed is as instantly certain about all of this as about a car without wheels.

To the two boys Ed said, "Remind me how long you're ready to wait before I let you get what you're after. Just because you came back here to bug me, I should tell the cops you left something in the car."

The taller boy smirked. "And maybe since they already looked and didn't find anything they'll think somebody else dropped it there. Like you." Ed decided the taller boy was a better spoken type of person; a good negotiator yet very respectful. "Let us get our stuff," the taller boy said, "and disperse this cloud of culpability hanging about you smelling like an old sheepskin coat."

Ed looked from the taller boy to the smaller. "It isn't a gun, is it?"

The smaller boy said, "Stop talking and just let us get it."

"I need to know in case it turns out the thing shot somebody. When the cops ask me, I don't want to stand there trying to convince them I didn't do it. Stuff like that's lousy for my self-image."

The taller boy said, "Image has nothing to do with what's involved here."

Ed's patience grew short. "The last smart-mouth kid I met wears dentures. When do we get to the part where you tell me just what it is?"

The smaller boy said, "This is all too deep for you, mister. Just let us get it." He turned and began to walk around the garage and the taller turned to follow. Over his shoulder the shorter boy added, "We could break in anytime when you're at work." Watching them, Ed felt a sudden vertigo, as if he was falling forward.

In the Luxembourg Garden, Ed and his beautiful wife embrace and kiss. Small children speaking perfect French run past them laughing. Broad, bright flower-blossoms lean heavily toward the darkly fecund earth. On the other side of an iron fence painted forest-green, four boys stop kicking a soccer ball to watch them pass. A small, round and carefully dressed older man pauses smiling and tips his hat. At Port Royal near Boul' Miche, Ed and his beautiful wife enter a café, sit at a small, round table beside the front window and hold hands.

"All right," Ed said to their backs patting his trouser-pocket looking for the car keys. "But one thing. Whatever it is, you got to show it to me. That's all!"

The taller boy stopped and turned. "This is not a situation that lends itself to negotiation. Anything you do funny won't be."

Ed stepped forward. "It's that good?"

"Anyway," the taller boy said as he waited for Ed to catch up, "we weren't smoking pot. That was the police just saying that, I swear." His chin just reached Ed's elbow.

Through the Parisian café's windows, Ed and his beautiful wife watch the darkening sky while the lights of the city brighten. Their cups of espresso finished, they walk slowly along Boul' Miche toward the Seine. Moving among university students from the Sorbonne, they are jostled and nudged toward the middle of the sidewalk. Envious young men watch them stop to kiss beside buildings, in entrances to shops, beside kiosks selling newspapers. At intersections they hold hands gliding through the current of hustling pedestrians.

Ed peeled back the dark green tarp and unlocked the car's door. The smaller boy climbed into the back seat. The taller boy got into the back-seat beside him and then made a place for Ed. With the door closed, the inside of the car reeked of mold and mildew. Obscured by the twilight behind the garage, Ed never saw where inside the car the thing came from. But suddenly the smaller boy was passing something to the taller boy. In the weak light the object seemed to glow a powder blue. When finally Ed got a good look at it, he laughed.

"Where the hell did you find it? It looks like a giant goddamn potato wrapped in aluminum foil." The glow shimmered, brightened and dimmed unevenly as if with an irregular pulse. "That's the goofiest thing I ever saw. How do you get it to make that light? And just where the hell did you get it, anyway?" The taller boy handed it to Ed. As large as it was, it weighed hardly anything. It seemed to hum quietly. Ed felt a slight electrical tingle vibrate in his hands. "What the hell is this thing?"

The taller boy said, "It's cool."

The smaller boy said, "It's from Mars."

"Right, sure, Mars," Ed said. "And you kids are nuts." Suddenly he was certain he was being fooled but he couldn't figure out how. "And so is this damn thing."

"What do you say, mister," the taller boy pleaded. "How about a little respect? That thing is very powerful. That thing could explode your head off. Like in this movie I saw."

"Yeah?" Ed said. "So what the hell does it do?"

"It puts things into your mind," the taller boy said. "Like visions, or movies."

"Yeah," the smaller boy said. "It's like having a tv inside your head."

Ed leaned back dreaming that he and his beautiful wife walk along Boulevard Saint Germain until they reach a small restaurant Ed knows well. The waiters stop to watch as the maître'd leads them to a table and they sit down. Their waiter appears immediately with menus which Ed ignores. Instead, he orders their entire meal in perfect French. This brings a smile to their waiter's face. Ed's beautiful wife glows, looking nowhere except at Ed. Later they finish their meals with cups of coffee. The waiters watch Ed pay their bill and stand. He takes the hand of his beautiful wife and guides her to the door, watched by every pair of eyes until they are gone. Ed enjoys eating, so he particularly likes this part of the dream.

The taller boy said, "Just hold it and stare at the light. You'll get pictures, I promise."

Ed held it and stared. The smaller boy said, "I don't always get pictures. But I like the sound it makes, too. It's kind of like music."

To the smaller boy, the taller said, "That's not music. That's just the buzzing and the voices of the people and stuff in the pictures. I get great pictures, all in funny colors." Turning to Ed he said, "But you got to stare at the light. And then the buzzing feels really cool on your fingers."

"The buzzing is very cool," the smaller boy said.

Ed asked, "What kind of pictures am I supposed to be getting?"

"You hear the music yet?" the smaller boy asked. "It's tough to pick up at first. Try to concentrate."

Ed closed his eyes. The boys watched. After a few moments Ed opened his eyes again. "Nothing," he said, "except the light and that damn buzzing in my fingers."

They walk slowly arm-in-arm back along Boulevard Saint Germain until they've returned to Boul' Miche. There they turn toward the roar of the traffic and nightlife swirling just beyond them. They pick their way along, stopping to look into a clothing shop, a jewelry shop, and a shop offering women's lingerie. They embrace and kiss at each stop so that it takes a while to pass along the boulevard. Finally at their backs stands the great statue of Saint Michael. Large yellow spotlights illuminate the saint astride the dragon with his great lance sinking deep into the beast's side. Hundreds of people swarm about, passing through the lurid, brilliant lights of the cafés surrounding them along with the headlights of cars. Ahead and illuminated with lights from below stands the cathedral of Notre Dame. Ed and his beautiful wife make their way across to Pont Saint Michele. Under the blue-black sky and with the Seine below them and cars passing beside them and Notre Dame towering over them they embrace and they kiss, long and passionately, while the noise disappears leaving only their breathing and the sweet pleasure of their lips. They stand pressed together nearly forever.

The smaller boy said, "The music is really great but the buzzing is the coolest part." Ed felt for a handkerchief to blow his nose but came up empty and decided against it.

The taller boy said, "Yeah, the coolest part is the buzzing. The pictures are neat and all, but the buzzing is the best." He reached toward Ed to take the object from his hands.

Ed pulled it back. "Let me give it another try." He held the object right up to his face, stared intently into the powdery blue light. "What I should do, I should relax."

"Yeah, there you go," the taller boy said. "Try to relax a little. Go with it. Give it a chance."

Ed sat very still, held the light almost to his eyes and refused to blink. After a moment he let his hands and the object drop into his lap. He squinted, his eyes closed. "Man, that's about to give me a headache. How the hell do you stand it?"

Ed realizes he's waiting for a train, and he should know something.

A man, a stranger, signals to Ed from the end of the train platform. Ed tries to scrape something that's become attached to the bottom of his shoe. He turns away to watch a train pull into the station. He is going by train to New York City and to a hotel where he will sleep with a woman named Stephanie. He scrapes his foot along the concrete appalled by what has become attached to his shoe, and can't remember if the woman is his wife.

The train to New York City is packed with travelers. Ed stands at the end of the car thinking only about what has become attached to his shoe. A middle-aged blond woman with a blond child on her hip tries to pass. He half-turns to give her more room.

Smiling she says, "Don't worry, he won't bite." One of the child's shoes falls off. Ed leans down and retrieves it. The child glances once at Ed and begins to cry, it's smooth, pink mouth opens wide as a snake's.

At the Café Car, Ed buys a small bottle of apple juice and then returns to his bags to drink it. When he's half-finished the apple juice, its slick, glass bottle slips from his fingers and when it hits the floor the remaining juice spills onto his shoes. It soaks his socks and his feet become wet with apple juice. Ed looks up to catch the glance of a man seated halfway along the car. He suspects this is the man from the platform. The man snaps his newspaper and raises it to cover his eyes. Ed tries to find the men's room but the train stops suddenly.

Ed gets off the train and looks up to see he is standing in Penn Station. Outside at the curb he sees the woman and child from the train standing on the sidewalk close by. She holds one of the child's shoes in her hand and turns frequently as if looking for someone. The child appears to be asleep. Ed flags down a cab.

Since it is Sunday, Ed asks the cab driver how the Giants are doing. The cab driver turns on him angrily. "What's with you guys? You think the whole damn world cares around your goddamn football? What the hell is it with guys like you?" They complete the journey in silence. When they reach the hotel Ed gives the driver a large tip.

Ed leaves his bags with the desk clerk to be brought up to his room. Through a doorway to the lounge he sees Stephanie already seated at a table. He recognizes her immediately. When he sits down she asks about his trip and then asks if he smells apples. He tells her about the crowded train and the apple juice, but not what he fears has become stuck to his shoe. She laughs and tells him his story is cute. He begins to tell her about the woman with the baby and the child's shoe. She asks if the child is a boy or a girl. Ed admits he didn't notice. Stephanie looks up at him as if surprised. He can no longer remember why he has begun this story.

Later over dinner they review the business meetings each will attend the next day. Each of their days are to be filled with meetings. These meetings seem important although Ed cannot remember why. He tells her he'll leave a message at the desk. Stephanie says she should leave a message as well.

During the night Ed dreams about the woman and the baby shoe. Except that there is no baby, although in this dream he and this woman know that the baby is nearby. In the dream he can't find the child's shoe and the woman is frantic to locate it, she gestures soundlessly but continually toward the baby who is not there.

Ed awakes suddenly to discover that Stephanie is no longer lying beside him. The light in the bathroom is on. Inside he sees that his and Stephanie's shoes are in the bathtub, but she is not there. The bathtub is half-filled with cold water. The shoes are obviously ruined. It is still gray morning. Ed wonders if she has gone to get more shoes. He wonders if he will ever see her again. He wonders if shoes left in a bathtub half-filled with water means something. He calls for room service and breakfast is sent up. Ed turns on the television to watch the news as he eats his breakfast.

Halfway through his breakfast Stephanie enters their room, a large shopping bag hangs from one hand. Tears black with her smeared mascara stream down either side of her face. She puts the bag down beside the bed, sits down in the chair across the breakfast tray from Ed and sighs. She then sips from his coffee cup and watches the television. Ed asks quietly about the shoes in the tub. Stephanie turns to him large-eyed with injured surprise. "I thought you put them there. As soon as I saw them I realized they were ruined. I need to make those meetings. I went out to buy more shoes."

"Did you buy shoes for me?" Ed asks.

"But you put them there. Why did you do such a horrible thing? Why do you hate me? What hideous mind could think up such a spiteful revenge? You know how much I love my shoes. You did it just to hurt me. You put the shoes in the tub because you hate me." She stands abruptly nearly knocking over the tray, slips on a pair of shoes from one of the boxes and leaves, slamming the door behind her.

Ed is not certain he hates her and seems more surprised by this accusation than she is. He calls down to room service. He showers and changes. Soon after, a pair of shoes is brought to him.

At lunch with a man he does not know, Ed accidentally leaves his appointment book on the restaurant table. A waiter bursts from the restaurant door just as Ed is getting into a cab. He hands Ed his appointment book and Ed hands the waiter a large tip. The waiter becomes angry and throws the money into the street. This confuses Ed.

He settles into the moving cab and opens the appointment book. In the lined calendar square for nine days ahead, a group of very small numbers fills its space. The numbers are arrayed as if forming an arithmetic problem. Except that the numbers do not add or subtract or multiply or divide. They could be identification numbers or model numbers or telephone numbers or even credit card numbers, but Ed knows these are not the type of numbers that combine to form greater or lesser numbers. Small and neat, they sit as carefully aligned as stacked poker chips. And Ed is certain he has not written them.

Before his next meeting, Ed realizes the shoes brought to him at the hotel are made of paper. He goes to a proper shoe store and buys two pairs of shoes but leaves them at the shop and arrives barefoot at his meeting five minutes late.

He retains no memory of this meeting, but at a table for dinner back at the hotel he waits one hour and twenty-eight minutes before Stephanie appears.

He realizes he's now wearing conventional leather shoes and this leaves him unaccountably happy. He has been drinking red wine until then, but orders coffee while they wait for their meal. Stephanie settles into her chair smiling. She says, "I love this city. Every time I come here I think the next time it'll be to move here once and for all. I love this place." From the tone of her voice and the smile on her lips and the way she shifts her hips while turning to look around, Ed is certain that Stephanie, who may or may not be his wife, has taken a lover in one of the large buildings she has gone into, and that she now sits across from him waiting only for the proper moment to leave.

Early the next morning Stephanie leaves their hotel room to drive a rented car north to her next appointment. Ed checks out of the hotel and takes the train headed south. He has appointments, all of them are elsewhere. The train is empty so he has no trouble finding a seat. Though he looks about frequently, he does not see anyone he recognizes. He does not wonder about Stephanie, but he is unhappy, and he slumps down in his seat wondering at its cause.

Ed suddenly felt the taller boy reach for the object. "Maybe it just isn't for you, mister." When he tried to take it, Ed gripped the object harder. "C'mon mister, just give it back."

In Paris, Ed and his beautiful wife begin their walk back along Boulevard Saint Germain and turn onto Boul' Miche. They are going to a jazz club Ed knows well. The second set is about to start and performing tonight is one of Ed's favorite piano-players. The group features a hot, young trumpet player Ed has recently heard about. The patrons all watch Ed and his beautiful wife take a small table to one side of the stage. A waiter hovers at Ed's elbow. At the end of the set the piano player points to their table and dedicates the last number to Ed's beautiful wife. It is gorgeous music and his beautiful wife takes his hand and squeezes it. Her eyes sparkle by the light of the candle. He sighs certain he has learned something.

Ed felt another tug and gripped the device in his hands tighter. He said, "Hey, give me a minute. Give me another chance. You said there was music."

"Sure," the smaller boy said. "Try it again. Maybe you'll pick up the music." The smaller boy reached behind his own back. "What you should do is hold the thing from underneath. Close your eyes and let your head drop back." Ed leaned his head back and closed his eyes. The door handle beside the smaller boy quietly clicked. He nudged the taller boy. The taller boy leaned closer to Ed. He got both hands around the thing just as Ed opened his eyes.

"Hey!" Ed said. He pulled at the object but the taller boy held tight. Ed jerked the object from the taller boy's hands, and it continued until it crashed into the door. The object broke into a dozen irregular pieces, its edges thin as eggshells; it was hollow and its light disappeared.

In a flash the taller boy smashed his fist into Ed's stomach. The smaller boy was instantly out the door, the taller boy behind him. Ed sat very still in the back-seat of his car waiting to catch his breath. He looked down to the pieces on the floor no longer thinking about Paris. The absence of his beautiful wife didn't bother him a bit. Despite the pain in his stomach he enjoyed a surge of relief, certain that all of it could have ended much worse and in ways he could hardly dream. But finally he could abandon the Charger and its false promise, its fairy-tale as a fraudulent dream, and released, that promise drifted from his fingers like wet smoke. Freed from the responsibility of dreaming, he was relieved that his nights were once again his own and he need share them with no one.

WAITING FOR THE WIDOW

THAT NIGHT, ARCHIE CALLED saying I should meet him at Lou's Iguana Steakhouse. I said, Lou makes lousy iguana steaks. Archie said, So don't eat them, but we still got to bury Izzy. I said, He's been in that meat locker a week already. What's the hurry? But Archie just hung up.

Alf, Randy, Too-Big and Princess were all sitting at a table in the back with Archie when I finally got to Lou's and all sharing the same cup of coffee. When he saw me Randy asked, You got any money? I turned out my pockets before I sat down. He shrugged and turned to Alf saying, I hang with the wrong types; you know what I'm saying? Too-Big said, You hang with the only types who would hang with you. Randy said, That's what I'm saying.

To Archie I asked, So where's Izzy?

Princess said, Izzy isn't, and then laughed.

Archie asked, How many times you going to make that joke?

Till I stop laughing at it, Princess said. She fluttered her eyes at Too-Big and said, Ask him.

Too-Big said, Nobody asks me nothing if they want to know something. He didn't turn to look at Princess.

To me Randy asked, You sure you don't have money?

I said, Didn't I show you my pockets?

How about that money you keep in your shoe, Alf said. I didn't answer that because the truth usually hurts.

Lou came to our table, a dirty rag hanging over his fat belly, and said, Get him out of my basement. That's all, just out.

I said, I'll have what they're having.

Lou said, It just ain't decent is all. Besides, I need the space.

Alf passed me the coffee cup. To Lou he said, Don't worry. Tonight, we promise. Lou grumbled as he walked away. To his back I asked, Kill any iguanas today?, but he just kept walking.

Randy asked, So, when do we start? Too-Big said, We're waiting for Leonard and the Widow. I asked, She's coming? Princess said, She's the widow, why not? Princess tapped long red-painted fingernails impatiently on the formica as she stared up at Too-Big. Irritating.

I said, If she's coming, I'm going.

To no one in particular Princess said, Coming and going, that's all these boys think about, and then she glanced again at Too-Big. He stared at his too-big hands that were clasped together on the table like wrestling bear cubs.

To Princess, Randy said, Just as long as they come, what's the difference to you?

Alf said, We got to let her come or Izzy wouldn't like it.

Besides, Randy said to me, you'll be glad to see her; she looks great.

Alf said, And don't worry. She's bringing Leonard with her so she won't bother you. Seems like both you and Izzy were easy to replace. Hearing all this didn't make me like iguana steaks any better.

Princess said, Izzy isn't, and laughed again.

Cut it out, Archie said.

I asked, So, where's he now? Who?, Alf asked. Guess, I said.

Alf said, Still in Lou's meat-locker.

Too-Big said, Probably likes it down there, next to all them frozen iguanas and all.

Princess shivered. She said, When I go, I want flowers.

Yeah, sure, Too-Big said. You got plans? I'll make a note.

What's that supposed to mean?, Princess asked half standing.

No fights, Archie said. Business now, fight later.

Later won't be soon enough, Princess said as she sat down again. We each took a sip from the coffee cup. To Too-Big, Princess said, You know I was only kidding.

Kidding about which?, Too-Big asked.

I said, We're going to carry a coffin, right? And to carry a coffin we need strength, right? So how do we get strong drinking this coffee?

Archie said, So take off a shoe and buy us a meal.

I asked, What about the Widow? It's her husband we're burying. Why don't she buy us a meal?

Randy said to Archie, He's got a point. Archie said, He's also probably got fifty bucks in his shoe, and here he's drinking our coffee.

I said, The coffee belongs to who drinks it.

Alf grabbed the cup and drank all the coffee down. I guess it's all mine now, he said with a resonant belch. Standing, Randy said, And who drinks it pays for it.

Archie said, Hey, you guys stop screwing around, right?

Too-Big said, Yeah, this is serious stuff. We got to get Izzy out of here and you guys act like it was just a big joke.

Yeah, Princess said, just a big, silly joke.

Archie said, Izzy isn't. Princess laughed.

I said, I don't think any of us is taking this all too very seriously.

Except him, Princess said nudging Too-Big.

And Izzy, Too-Big said.

Randy said, That's because he owed you money.

Alf asked, Who didn't Izzy owe money to? Nobody said anything and then the Widow came in followed by Leonard. We all stood as they came toward the table.

Tough break, Alf said shaking her hand. Randy shook her hand saying, Really sucks. Archie said, Couldn't have happened to a better guy. My turn was next and I said, He was a genuine prince. Princess kissed her on the cheek saying, He was a great lay, I'll bet. Then Too-Big shook her hand asking, You got any money? Leonard stepped forward and put a five-dollar bill on the table. Too-Big glanced at it and said, That's a start.

The Widow said, If Izzy was here he'd be happy to see you all together to walk his last mile.

But Izzy isn't, Princess said and laughed but then caught herself.

Actually he's right down stairs, Alf said.

Archie waved at Lou who came to our table. Archie said, Coffee all around, and then handed the five-dollar bill to Lou. He glared at us wiping his hands on the greasy rag at his belt before he took it and walked away.

Actually, it's more like two and a quarter, I said.

Leonard said, What? I said, Miles. Leonard just looked at me so I said, To the graveyard. Two and a quarter miles. Everyone was quiet so I said, And then there's that coffin. It isn't just Izzy. He was a skinny guy. To Randy I said, You know what I mean? Real skinny.

But all this time I couldn't keep my eyes off the Widow. She crouched in my mind like a sore tooth, inflamed and shimmering with a fire that came on in waves.

Randy finally nodded saying, Couldn't have been more than one-twenty-five.

The Widow said, Closer to one-fifty. He'd been putting on weight.

Bet that was you, Princess said, feeding him and all. He really liked his iguana steaks.

Too-Big nodded saying, Always bumming money to buy another iguana steak.

And you always lent the money to him, the Widow said. Her eyes brimmed for an instant. You were all great friends to him, she said.

He was so annoying, Alf said, you'd give him anything just to get him off you.

The Widow sighed saying, How well I remember. Princess sighed saying, Me too.

I said, So it's the coffin that'll be tough to carry. Just talking to hear my own voice and maybe to get the Widow's attention. The tooth-pain burned and swelled, like being in a boat rocking at anchor under a really hot sun.

Leonard said, Don't worry, I have my van outside. Besides, in his own funny way Izzy was sort of a saint and I admired him.

The Widow said, Shut up, Leonard. And Archie said, Yeah, Leonard, shut up. And Princess said, Yeah, just shut up. Too-Big said, And you shut up too, to Princess. And Princess said, Who are you telling to shut up? Too-Big said, How many people at this table named Princess. Princess stood and was about to say something when the Widow said to her, I'm really glad you're here with me. And I know that Izzy is, too. Princess said, Izzy isn't, and laughed.

Randy asked, Shouldn't we get started? It's already after midnight.

Too-Big said, Izzy ain't in any hurry. Besides, he's probably pretty happy down there what with all that iguana meat.

All you ever think of, Princess said, is meat. Archie said, That ain't what you said last night.

Princess said, I don't have to sit here and take this abuse.

Randy said, So stand up.

The Widow said, Everybody has to be nice to Princess. At least tonight.

Everybody's always nice to Princess, Alf said. That's the problem.

Leonard said, Just leave Princess alone. Alf and Randy said, Shut up, Leonard, at the same time. To Leonard, Princess said, You don't have to shut up if you don't want to. I like to hear your voice.

To Leonard, Alf said, You're in trouble now.

Archie said, Randy's right, we should get this show on the road. Lou waddled to our table with his tray of hot coffees.

Archie said, Listen Lou, mind if we bury Izzy with one of your iguana steaks? On the house, I mean? Just for old-time sake. Too-Big said, Him being such a good customer and all. Lou looked around at the table and shrugged. Sure, Lou said, just get him out of here. But only one, okay? Even you guys can count that high.

The Widow said, You're a prince, Lou.

Here's mud in you cup, Archie said and drank his coffee.

Too-Big pushed his coffee away saying, You're a cheap sonofabitch, Lou, but for Izzy's sake we'll take the just one.

Alf said, He really loved your iguana steaks. Lou rubbed his hands on the dirty rag at his belt saying, You guys are full of shit. Just get Izzy out of my basement. I close in another hour. Lou turned and started back toward the kitchen.

To his back Too-Big said, Cheap and lazy. Lou kept walking but over his shoulder he said, Nobody pays me to keep stiffs in my locker. One hour. Randy said, Tell that to the iguanas, but not loud enough for Lou to hear.

Lou's right, Leonard said. He isn't getting any fresher down there. I said, Shut up, Leonard, but nobody said anything else. We all drank coffee.

Alf said, Least we could do is get him into the coffin. Randy said, But we can't get the coffin into the freezer. Too-Big asked, So what? Randy said, So we'd have to get him out of here then. Archie said, Randy's right. We take him out of that freezer, he's going to start to thaw out. Then he's going to really stink. I asked, So we really ain't going to bury Izzy tonight?

Archie said, I only said we'd try to bury Izzy tonight.

I said, So how about we give it a real shot.

Too-Big said, Don't you listen too good? If we screw up he's going to stink.

Leonard said, I don't think we should have this conversation with the Widow right here.

Shut up, Leonard, the Widow said. Besides, we're going to bury Izzy tonight. Isn't that right? The rest of us drank more coffee.

That's why I'm here, I said to the Widow.

I thought it was for your scintillating conversation, Princess asked.

Randy said, He thinks the Widow is here because of him. Randy spoke the truth again; more pain. Leonard said, We're here because we're going to bury Izzy. Princess said, Shut up, Leonard, but then made this weird-for-Princess laugh.

Archie said, We owe it to Izzy. Am I right?

When you're right, the Widow said, there's nothing more to say.

Palms flat on the table Too-Big asked, So what do we say?

To Leonard, Randy asked, You got any more money? I could use another cup of coffee before we go at this. Leonard glanced at the Widow and then pulled another five out of his pocket and laid it on the table. For the first time since the two of them came in I was glad I wasn't Leonard.

Archie said, Hey Lou, another round of coffees.

The Widow said, Sorry, Leonard, sometimes I forget why I invite you places. After a while Lou came with the tray of hot coffees. He asked, Remember your friend? He's still in my basement.

Alf asked, You sure or you just guessing?

Lou said, Now you got a half hour.

Randy said to me, One thing you can say about Lou, he's good with clocks. I said, One of the best. Too-Big said, Can't cook for shit, but he's handy with a clock. Archie said, Lou's got a point, and here you guys are making fun of him.

Randy said, Not me. I said, Not me. Too-Big asked, So what?

Alf asked, So when do we get Izzy?

Princess said, Izzy isn't, and laughed. We drank more coffee. Then Princess began to pout. She said, Look, I got important things to do. Randy said, Anybody we know? Princess ignored him saying, I ain't got all night is all.

Archie said, She's right, we came here for a reason. He stood saying, I'm going down the basement. Who else is coming? Too-Big stood saying, Finally, we're going to get some action.

Princess said, That's not what you said last night.

I stood, too. Randy stood saying, No point putting this off. Alf stood and then Leonard stood. The Widow stood saying to Leonard, You stay here, precious. I don't want you getting your hands dirty. To Leonard the Princess said, Keep me company, and smiled. It was one of her better smiles. Leonard sat down.

Single file with Archie in the lead and the Widow at the end we walked to the back of Lou's and reached the door to the cellar. Down narrow dark stairs and then we stood together in Lou's basement in front of the big metal door to the meat-locker. The dark wooden coffin lay stretched across two saw-horses to one side, the lid was propped open and it was empty. Archie said, Who's going in? Too-Big said, We'll all go in. Alf said, Except for the Widow. The Widow said, I'm going too; he's my husband.

Past tense, Randy said.

Husbands are forever, the Widow said.

Archie lifted the big latch on the metal door and pulled it open. One weak light-bulb burned high on the wall at the back. Pale fog filled the chamber, obscuring the gray frozen iguana steaks hanging like stalactites from hooks in the ceiling and stacked on the concrete floor like chopped white wood.

Randy asked, So where did we put him?

Alf said, In the back; I think over there. He began to walk. We bumped our heads on the hard hanging steaks, tripped over their stacks obscured in the weak light.

Randy asked, You sure? Too-Big asked, What's to be sure? He swatted at a steak hanging before his eyes. After a while Alf said, Maybe we put him over there, and moved toward the other corner.

Randy said, Maybe Lou got a shipment of steaks and had to move him.

Too-Big said, He would have told us. He would have said, Hey, I had to move your buddy, he was in my way.

Randy said, That's Lou for you; moves your buddy's corpse and don't even tell you.

We began to wander; eyes searched the floor, the corners. We'd come upon each other in the fog and then drift apart, disappear, meet up again and move on.

Finally Archie said, Listen, something's wrong here. Only so many places you can hide a corpse in a place this big.

Alf asked, You think he ain't here?

Did you find him?, Archie asked. Alf didn't say anything. Archie asked, Did anybody find him? No one spoke. Archie said, Seems we have what you call your inescapable conclusion.

The Widow said, Maybe Lou moved him to somewhere else in the basement.

Too-Big said, Lou's that kind of guy; meat's always in the way.

We left the locker and closed the door. The rest of the cellar was small; in no time we'd searched every corner.

Randy said, Holy shit, what'll we do now?

Too-Big said, We ask Lou what he did with Izzy.

The Widow said, Izzy isn't. She didn't laugh

Alf asked, You think Lou'd send us down here if he already knew Izzy was gone?

I asked, What sense does this make? That Izzy came back to life, sneaked out of the basement and walked away?

Too-Big said, Something just ain't right.

Randy said, We got to do something.

We were all quiet for a time. Then Archie said, Tell you what. Let's close the coffin, carry it up the stairs like we're carrying Izzy and get the hell out of here.

Just then Lou's voice came from the top of the cellar stairs asking, You gonna be much longer down there?

Archie yelled, On our way up.

Randy whispered, But we got to find Izzy. We can't just leave him.

Alf said, You think of any place we ain't looked, you go and look there and let us know what you find.

I said, I'm with Archie. We close the casket and get out of here.

Too-Big said, I'm with Randy; we can't leave Izzy here.

Alf said, Wherever Izzy is, he ain't down here and we are. I say we close the box and go. He turned to the Widow saying, But it's your call.

She only hesitated a second. She said, Let's close up the casket and go.

And so we did.

Upstairs, Lou stood beside the front door leaning on his broom. He asked, What took you all so long?

Randy said, We had respects to pay. Not like you'd know anything about that.

As we stood with the coffin, the Widow stepped up to Lou and kissed him lightly on the cheek. She said, Thanks, Lou. Izzy spent many happy hours with you. I know a part of him will always be here.

Lou unlocked the front door saying, Just not too much of him. But he was a good guy, it was a tough break.

Too-Big asked, Hey, where's Princess?

Lou said, Left ten minutes ago while you all were saying good-bye. Her and that other guy.

In unison, Too-Big and the Widow both said, No shit!

For no good reason I could figure my spirits suddenly improved.

We carried the coffin out and Lou locked up behind us. Randy asked, Now what'll we do?

The Widow said, Leonard's van is around the corner.

Alf said, But Leonard's gone.

The Widow smiled. Not with his van, she said. A ring of keys clattered brightly in her hand.

We loaded the coffin into the back of the van and climbed in behind it. Archie got behind the wheel and Too-Big rode shot-gun. Randy, Alf, the Widow and me rode in the back on either side of the empty coffin. I tried to get the Widow's attention, make eye contact, but in the shadows who could tell?

Randy said, I don't know what makes me feel worse; Izzy's coffin, or Izzy's coffin without Izzy.

Archie asked, Where to?

The Widow said, Drive to Jersey. We'll dump the coffin. Lots of woods in Jersey.

Alf asked, Where in Jersey?

The Widow asked, Is there a where in Jersey?

Too-Big said, Widow's got a point.

We crossed the bridge and drove another half hour into some woods. Archie found a dirt road and followed it deeper into the woods, killed the lights and stopped with the motor running. Too-Big hopped out and came around while I opened the back doors. Randy and I stood to lift the coffin, but Too-Big said, I got it. He pulled the coffin from the van, lifted it high over his head and at a run disappeared to the sound of crashing tree-branches into the woods. A few minutes later we all heard the coffin crash to the ground and then Too-Big reappeared brushing his hands together. As he leaned into the back of the van to close the back doors the Widow asked, How come everybody calls you Too-Big? Too-Big paused, hesitated and then smiled, the first time he'd smiled all night. He locked the doors, got back into his seat beside Archie. Archie put the van in gear. Alf said, Seems like a waste of a good coffin.

Archie asked, You want we should go back and get it for you? Maybe you got somebody in mind?

The Widow said, Never too many coffins.

Too-Big said, Score another for the Widow. He turned to her and smiled again. She smiled back. My chest emptied, it was time to go home, time to be alright.

We drove back across the bridge and stopped in a street a couple of blocks from Lou's. Archie said, End of the road. We all got out and the Widow moved up into the driver's seat. She said, Thanks for all the help. I couldn't have done this myself.

Randy asked, But what happened to Izzy?

Archie said, I ain't going back to ask Lou. How about you? Nobody said anything. Then to Too-Big the Widow said, I could use some company while I find a place to park this thing. Too-Big got into the passenger seat. I had to smile; there was nothing else to do, so I didn't do it. We watched from the sidewalk as the van drove away.

Alf shook his head asking, How do you ask a guy what he did with your buddy's corpse?

Archie said, I been thinking. You know how Lou always has all that meat hanging around in his locker?

Nobody could think of anything worth saying after that until Randy said, That Lou's a funny guy. After that we all said our good-nights. The sky had begun to brighten and eventually we found our ways home. A month later Too-Big and the Widow got married. Nobody ever saw Leonard or the Princess again. I still see the others from time to time but I never went back to Lou's.

And I'll never, ever, eat another iguana steak again.

BRIAN'S UNEMPLOYMENT MONKEY

BRIAN HAD BEEN LAID-OFF BEFORE, and although the occurrence still left him furious, he knew the drill; the call into the HR office ostensibly for a brief meeting only to find papers already drawn up and spread on the desk merely needing his signature. He leaned forward to put his name to something he wasn't expected to read while the HR expert brought in for just this task explained that his layoff was necessary for the continued survival of the company and did not reflect on Brian's performance. And then she added that, yes, his application for unemployment benefits would not be challenged. Seeing his relief she smiled and wished Brian very best of luck with his future, and then volunteered to accompany him back to his desk to collect whatever had personal significance to Brian which had not been paid for by the company. And because Brian has always been mistrustful about jobs he has never left anything personal at his desk and so this step in an otherwise humiliating process happily took no time at all. From his desk she then escorted him to the elevator where once again she offered best-of-luck wishes and then reminded him not to forget his monkey. Yes, Brian had been here before and expected eventually to be here again. But he was puzzled by the monkey.

At the elevator the HR expert explained that his new monkey didn't have a name, and Brian's first task was to give one to it to personalize it and thereby encourage its enthusiasm and loyalty. The monkey, she further explained, had been trained and educated at a prestigious university especially to assist those like Brian engaged in a job-search. This monkey, she assured Brian, would quickly peruse the Internet each day in search of employment opportunities which fit Brian's employment profile and then submit an application for him. All of this assistance would free Brian to pursue those networking opportunities he was assured were necessary for any successful job search. Thus, all that Brian needed was to have his updated resume and cover letter copied to a folder on his computer's desktop, because after that, even a monkey could complete his job applications. Once his monkey was comfortable behind Brian's computer, Brian simply needed to keep an eye on his e-mail and a freshly dry-cleaned suit hanging in the closet because a blizzard of job offers undoubtedly would soon pour in.

The monkey presented to Brian at his employers' elevator was attached to a leather leash linked to a collar which the monkey appeared to resent. Two and a half feet tall with mostly dark fur but with tan fur on his chest, the monkey looked up with large and glistening eyes turning from one to the other as if following the conversation between Brian and the HR person. When Brian finally looked down in acknowledgment of his new and furry companion, the monkey returned his look with a wide, large-toothed grin, as if he was as embarrassed and as dubious of all this as Brian but otherwise was optimistic the two of them would become friends.

Brian suspected the monkey's was an expression that also included pity and contempt. Upon being first introduced, Brian had been inclined to speak to the monkey, perhaps say hello or introduce himself or simply ask how this monkey was doing. Instead, he gently tugged on the leash. This gesture triggered a snarl from the monkey and Brian made a mental note to refrain from repeating that in the future. The HR person stood beside the elevator grinning with fraudulent optimism as the elevator doors closed.

Descending together with his new monkey within the elevator, Brian fumed. After all, he had found jobs before over the years and never needed the help of a monkey. So he wondered if this gift in fact was some critical comment about his competency as an adult; was he being told he had become too old, or that he was not sufficiently current on the latest technology and that he hadn't kept sufficiently up? Even worse, since this monkey had been given to him without charge, was he being told this was it and he'd never find another job without it?

The monkey's presence with its suggestion of his incompetence annoyed him into a grumbling resentment all the way down to the ground floor.

At the curb in front of the office of his most recent employer and on this his first afternoon of being unemployed, Brian hailed a taxi cab. When it pulled to the curb, his monkey nonchalantly climbed in and sat quite still on the back seat of the cab beside Brian. Relieved by this suggestion of civility, Brian took the opportunity to review those papers he had been handed and they arrived at his apartment without incident. He opened the front door of his apartment wondering how all of this was likely to turn out. But that question disappeared when the monkey unhooked his collar from the leash and dashed into Brian's bathroom. And he was ecstatic when the monkey closed the bathroom door behind him. Then and there he decided to call this monkey Albert, because clearly this was some kind of monkey Einstein.

Brian's separation documents included three full pages specifically regarding this monkey he had named Albert including a list of those foods Albert preferred, and he was reassured that every food listed could be purchased at his local grocery store. But the documents also informed him that Albert would only work for Brian for eight hours each day, and only Monday through Friday. Outside these hours Brian was encouraged to provide his monkey with entertainment. Brian found this instruction both vague and startling. After all, he had no idea what would entertain a monkey except another monkey. Finally, the document informed him that Albert would assist his job search until Brian accepted an offer of employment.

When Albert emerged from the bathroom he scampered around Brian's apartment until he spotted Brian's desktop computer. Brian decided that Albert was an especially brilliant monkey because unlike many of the humans he knew he was instantly able to figure out how to turn on his computer. Albert watched the computer boot-up, and when the desktop appeared on the screen he used the mouse to search for Brian's documents. It occurred to Brain that the monkey was trying to find copies of his resume and cover letter. But when he gestured to take over the mouse, Albert began to screech, seemingly incensed by the implied insult to his monkey intelligence. Confident that Albert would eventually turn and appeal for his help, Brian backed away. But he was astonished when Albert not only found his application documents, but then using the mouse and keyboard he created a new folder on the desktop, labeled that folder "Employment" and then pasted those documents within.

Brian was not surprised that Albert was a slow typist, but he was impressed that Albert's typing was grammatically accurate.

Brian now found himself perplexed by what seemed to him to be an ambiguous relationship. On the one hand, theirs was a formal relationship in that there were responsibilities each was expected to fulfill. But their co-habitation as described in the documents seemed to imply a casual partnership of sorts. Brian wondered how they would navigate that terrain, especially as one member of this partnership was inarticulate. He considered augmenting the list of rules with a few of his own invention and he was even prepared to discuss them with Albert in the hope that the monkey would participate willingly.

Once Albert had the computer to himself he opened the Internet browser and using the keyboard and mouse located eight web sites offering employment opportunities. Brian was baffled by how the creature managed all of this, and he speculated that Albert had somehow learned to recognize English language words. But he was stunned when Albert negotiated all the steps needed to post his resume on each of those websites. Although this seemed absurdly unlikely, Albert then surveyed each of those websites for opportunities appropriate to Brian's resume. Despite his incredulity, Brian began to suspect that Albert might actually succeed in finding him a job.

All of this effort to find a new job for him pleased Brian, yet he remained uncomfortable. This creature clearly possessed skills similar to Brian's and he could not imagine how Albert managed this. Besides, Brian had always carried out his own job search and his employment history documented a consistent though middling success. So, impressed as he was by Albert's tricks, he wondered again and more deeply why those above him were certain he needed this monkey's assistance. He studied Albert from behind the monitor as the monkey stared intently while moving the mouse and then clicking. Albert did all of this with a level of concentration Brian conceded he would have found difficult to sustain. In the end Albert appeared to have Brian's job search under control, so he decided he might as well watch some tv.

Brian switched to a tv program he found sufficiently distracting and watched for some minutes although his mind was elsewhere, drifting around that job he had just lost and those jobs he'd had in the past and how they had been found and how they had been lost. So it took some time for him to realize that Albert had been staring at the monitor and yet was remarkably quiet.

Silently Brian stood and stepped away from the tv, and then from over

Albert's shoulder he glanced at the monitor. To his astonishment he saw images on the screen of humans engaging in sex. Albert's monkey-sense somehow alerted him to Brian's presence because with a sudden movement of the mouse Albert returned the screen to Brian's job search. He turned and looked up then to face Brian with a toothy embarrassed grin, as if promising this would not happen again.

Baffled but determined to avoid a conflict with his monkey, Brian returned to his chair and the tv but he could not quiet his own astonishment. While his tv program played, Brian sorted through what he had just seen. He was astonished it was even possible that a monkey might find photographs of humans engaging in sex exciting. It seemed intuitively true that Albert would find photos of monkeys engaging in sex far more fascinating than any such photos involving humans. What could there be about photos of humans that might excite a monkey? Brian considered the question for some time before deciding to check the computer and see exactly which photos Albert found most interesting.

Cautiously approaching the monitor, he was again startled to see from over the monkey's shoulder more images similar to the ones Albert had opened before. But Albert must have anticipated Brian's appearance this time because the images disappeared in a flash, replaced by links to job opportunities. Albert again turned to Brian grinning, as if to insist he was doing his job. His grin seemed sincere as if he hoped to appeal to Brian's sympathy and solidarity; as if to say that, after all, we're all only monkeys, and monkeys is all we'll ever be. But Brian's confusion deepened. Unable to disentangle these variously knotted veils of perplexity obscuring his understanding, he concluded that his was simply an exceptionally clever monkey who he was unlikely to fool, so he returned to his tv and waited until Albert left his chair to pay another visit to the bathroom.

Brian listened until he heard the bathroom door close and then he stood and moved to the computer. The monkey had left the Internet browser open, and Brian opened the browser's history. To his astonishment he discovered that Albert had somehow managed to erase that entire document. He tried those few tricks he knew attempting to recover that history when he heard the toilet flush and then the bathroom door open. He returned to the screen Albert had left open, but finding Brian at the computer, Albert began to screech as though annoyed. Brian considered lying to Albert about what he'd been doing, but Albert seemed unlikely to listen to anything he said until Brian stood and returned control of the computer to him. Silently furious, Brian returned to his couch and the tv but now far more annoyed than intrigued.

Staring at the tv screen, Brian wondered if this was simply the opening salvo in a battle over control of his computer. Then he recalled that according to the documents, Albert would only engage in his job search until 5 PM. Brian assumed that afterward, the computer would be returned to his control so he decided to wait until then and avoid a battle with a monkey.

Time passed as Brian sat before his tv distracted, annoyed and brooding, and briefly he even dozed, but eventually 5 PM arrived. He stood from his chair relieved as if some sort of vigil was finally over and addressed Albert to the effect that it was quitting time and that he wanted to use the computer for his own purposes. But instead of conceding the computer to Brian, Albert stood on the chair and began screeching and jumping up and down as if to insist the computer remained in his control. Albert bared huge incisors in fury when Brian reached for the mouse. When Brian flinched and backed away, Albert then opened screen after screen of images of humans engaged in sex as if defiant of whatever Brian wanted. Brian became angry and demanded that Albert allow him to use his own computer. When he again gestured toward the mouse, Albert screeched furiously and tried to bite Brian's wrist. Only Brian's marginal agility kept the monkey from succeeding.

Frustrated, Brian took the paper stating the terms of Albert's employment and pointed out to the monkey that after 5 PM he was off the clock, and so Brian could resume using the computer. But snarling in response to what Brian said, Albert snatched the paper from his hands and stabbed with a crooked finger at that paragraph on the sheet before returning it to his grasp. Brian scrutinized the paragraph Albert had pointed to and discovered that it outlined Albert's off-time activities and included the phrase, "whatever he wants."

Brian now recognized himself as trapped. Until he accepted an offer of employment, Albert would retain control of this computer. Suddenly and despite all that he understood, he found himself wondering if he was capable of outsmarting an extremely smart monkey. After further reflection he began seriously to worry.

He needed to find a job quickly, because this monkey would fight him over use of the computer until then, and that prospect left Brian furious but also vaguely terrified. But it occurred to him that this might be part of Albert's training; that the monkey's annoying and aggressive behavior was calculated to hurry Brian in his job-search. This seemed redundant of course since being forced to share his life as well as his computer with a monkey seemed more than sufficient compulsion. Albert's computer search for those explicit photos felt almost gratuitous to Brian, as if it might even have been outside the monkey's training. But then it occurred to Brian that with all of this he was being told that he must take any job that was available and would accept him, regardless of wage or experience. So Brian now wondered if he had been labeled a trouble-maker, or worse some sort of slacker? Was he now regarded as a hopeless job-hopper; had his range of skills and years of experience become a valueless burden and even a disability, as if the more he had learned and had experienced the less useful he had made himself? Did all that he knew now make it unlikely he would find useful work because his work experience had in fact reduced his value to his community?

Brian suddenly noticed that Albert had been making quiet yet high-pitched sounds, and he stood. When he reached the computer he saw with a nauseating discomfort that Albert was enthusiastically masturbating. Albert looked up at Brian grinning without embarrassment and did not even slow down. Brian realized at that moment that some limit had been reached and then exceeded. Once again he brought out his discharge papers to see if anything there referred to Albert's intimate behavior. He found nothing specific to what Brian had witnessed but he was reminded that he needed to provide Albert with some sort of bed, although the papers were specific that the bed did not need to be more than a pillow and blanket. Conceding to the inevitable although slightly nauseous, from his closet Brian brought out a pillow and blanket and tossed both onto the floor beside the computer. He wondered then about sleeping in the same apartment with a monkey. He decided to lock the door to his bedroom and hope for the best.

As Albert continued to make those sounds that Brian now refused to think about, Brian watched the tv desperate for distraction. In this way he passed a remarkably distressing evening. But finally midnight approached, and Brian assumed his responsibilities for the day had reached an end. He turned off the tv and stood. Passing the computer he saw that Albert remained busy as he had been earlier and he gasped at the apparently limitless exuberance of Nature. Almost as a reflex he announced that he was going to bed and wished Albert goodnight. Albert did not even look up to watch him leave. Brian shook his head as he closed and locked the door to his bedroom, convinced he would have a lousy night's sleep. The night proved he was not wrong.

Brian awoke early the following morning and emerged from his bedroom to find Albert already awake and at the computer. He glanced down at the blanket and pillows wondering if Albert had slept at all and what he had done if he hadn't. As the instructions had explained, Brian brought pieces of fruit out of the refrigerator and placed them on the table beside Albert. The monkey devoured all of it quickly and left a pile of rinds and bits of partially eaten fruit whose size impressed Brian. This was another element of their co-habitation his document had not warned him about.

With breakfast disposed of, Brain saw that it was just past 9 AM and, sure enough, Albert was already at the computer engaged in Brian's job-search. And to Brian's surprise, Albert opened the email browser and then opened an email which offered Brian an interview for a position that Albert had submitted an application for. Albert jumped up and down gleefully on the computer chair as if proud of what he had accomplished. To Brian's surprise, Albert then moved aside as if inviting him to print-out the email and then key-in a response agreeing to the interview appointment. Brian read the job-description and was dismayed to discover it was a shipping-clerk's position paying less than half of what his previous position had paid. Brian's interior debate began; if he accepted this job he would loose his unemployment benefits and reduce his chances for a better-paying and more interesting job. So even though he was ready to accept the offer of this interview, finally he concluded that he owed it to himself to keep looking, and so he leaned over the keyboard. Albert watched the screen as Brian keyed-in his request to cancel the interview. When these words appeared on the screen Albert began to screech and scream and again he moved as if to attack Brian.

Brian explained to Albert what he planned to do and why, but Albert snatched up the sheets pertaining to his role in Brian's job-search and waved them at Brian. When he looked closely he read the words "accept the first legitimate offer". This dictate annoyed Brian more than anything else he found there. He looked at Albert a long moment before he decided he would not hold himself answerable to a monkey, and despite Albert's attempt to interfere, Brian keyed-in the interview cancellation and then hit Send. Albert studied Brian with an expression that blended fury with contempt. Brian attempted again to explain to the monkey what he had done and why, but Albert simply turned back to the computer screen and returned to those websites providing those photos he seemed to enjoy so much.

Brian debated with himself how best to proceed, but nothing became clear. For the moment he would ignore Albert's internet habits and concentrate instead on making certain of his interview offers. Of course, until Albert was ready to allow Brian to use his computer that was a plan he needed to postpone. Then suddenly, Brian noticed that his printer was operating. He stood and discovered in the printer's tray a small stack of about a half-dozen job opportunities which Albert had apparently applied to for Brian. When the printer stopped, Brian lifted the stack from the tray and flipped through skimming each job description. He was startled to discover at the bottom of the stack black & white copies of several of the types of images that Albert found so intriguing. Brian separated these from the job opportunities and waved them toward Albert, who grinned with embarrassment and then snatched them from Brian's hands.

Albert returned his attention to the computer screen while Brian looked more closely at the job descriptions. At first he was startled that every one of them paid less than the job he'd just been deprived of. Something must be seriously wrong. He had never made much money but he had always earned enough to cover his expenses. But these salaries were all disastrously low and being paid at these rates would force him to move far out of town. He conceded that losing one's job created many financial problems, but accepting one of these low-paying jobs would be ruinous. It was time, Brian decided, that he and Albert had a long talk.

Brian was optimistic that, considering how thoroughly-trained Albert was, and how clearly superior the monkey was mentally, he would succeed in convincing Albert to modify his job-search, and search only for jobs that paid about as much as his last job. But he found Albert staring so urgently at the images on the computer screen it took more than a moment to get his attention. With those pages of job descriptions in one hand, he pointed to each salary line and explained that if the number listed there was too small he could not accept the job. He studied Albert then, trying to determine if he had been understood.

Albert pawed through the sheets of paper and then turned to Brian screeching and hoping up and down on his chair. Then he jumped down to the floor and scampered to where Brian kept his discharge papers. He returned to Brian clutching one of the sheets and waved it at Brian making whining sounds. When Brian finally read the sheet he located the words 'whatever position is offered'. Albert then hoped back onto the chair and returned his attention to the computer screen and his photos.

Brian recognized his quandary. By accepting the first job offered, he risked losing his apartment. He realized he could expect no help from Albert after all. He returned to his couch before the tv drifting slowly downward into despair.

Near mid-day he brought out more fruit from the refrigerator and put it out beside Albert. But instead of abandoning the computer to enjoy his lunch, Albert ate as he continued to use the computer. Brian's despair bloomed and blossomed as he sank deeper.

Then, late in the afternoon Albert began to screech drawing Brian to the computer. To Brian's frustration, his email displayed a message inviting him to another interview. When he reviewed its original job posting he discovered it also paid far less than his previous job. He was tempted again to cancel this interview, but recalling Albert's previous reaction he hesitated. As he thought about it, he concluded that he could accept the interview and mess it up in such a way that he would never be offered this job and Albert would be no wiser. None of this made Brian feel better, but fooling this monkey offered a chance to hold onto his unemployment benefits and his apartment.

Brian recognized Albert's approval as he keyed-in his acceptance of this interview. He assumed that Albert would now return to his preferred website. But to his surprise Albert opened a screen to an on-line gambling site. Brian watched mildly amused as Albert engaged in one hand of Blackjack after the next, sometimes wagering large amounts of money, and nearly always losing. This continued for some time until Albert suddenly abandoned the computer and dashed to the bathroom.

With Albert now preoccupied Brian decided to look into Albert's wins and losses. And as he feared, Albert was a compulsive card player and lost far more often than he won. Brian felt himself smile. Probing further he opened the screen that displayed the information for Albert's on-line gambling account. His amusement turned to horror when he discovered that Albert was gambling using Brian's credit card. At that moment, Brian recognized that the light was now shining on him, and he could not step away.

THE VISITATION

THE LARGEST PART of our difficulty was the fact that none of us could decide how to feel. Even after breaking the event into discreet moments, each of which should have conjured a feeling to give it shape and color and even an aroma, with that absence of our feelings we could know nothing. And this is because feeling is reality so that there is no reality without feeling.

Thus that series of events which elaborated before us remained incomplete and unreal until our feelings, like tendrils of a vine that supports a collapsing wall, somehow had become attached to them. These events had occurred and therefore had existed and yet they amounted to less than nothing until our feelings had given them an interior architecture. As for those other parts of our difficulty which stymied me, I can't remember them. They were probably important, but just not important enough to remember.

Still, we knew that something had happened, some large thing of weight and depth. The questions which remained were the how and the why and the what-next. But the most important question obscured all of the others; how did we feel about it?

Several of our townsfolk had watched it the first time and instantly shook their heads certain that since it could not exist, it didn't. They returned to their lives determined to behave as if even if that occurrence had occurred, it was best not to speak of it. Yet after the third occurrence we were compelled to admit to each other that if this was our communal hallucination, it might become real regardless of our intentions otherwise.

My wife and I watched it the last two times it appeared, as vaguely threatening as heat lightening on the horizon. But just as everyone else did, we shrugged it off. I suspect this says something about our relationship; about our failure to explore each other's dreams. I hasten to add that it hadn't always been this way.

In the old days we described to each other our dreams from the previous night with a competitive thrill, always relishing their granular friability, as if those dreams might evaporate with the first glancing blow of speech. We believed that our selves experienced genuine feelings within these dreams, so there was some purpose beyond pleasure in charting their evolution. We discovered that our dreams could only be viewed from an angle and just managed to achieve substance through indirection. Optimistic they could be captured in their most eloquent contours, we once bought a large pad of newsprint determined to draw those things which had visited us during the night. To our surprise, this had turned out to be a lot of work and its sour effort lasted less than a week. But once it had been like that between us, and I mourn the passing of those days as being merely the dreams of dreams.

When finally we all agreed that something was out there just beyond the edge of our horizon we organized an expedition that gathered several of the more adventurous of our town in order to investigate. Our caravan of cars and trucks formed just after daybreak. Before departure we warned each other sternly to take no make-out detours, sex being an unavoidable distraction. The mayor and the police chief along with her deputy led our caravan. We were wary of their leadership however since they were notorious for their heavy-petting sessions conducted in broad daylight in the donut shop parking lot near the edge of town. Delightful as those excursions undoubtedly were, this was not the time for frivolous enjoyments and cheap pleasures. Our mission was earnest and urgent.

We drove quite a way and far enough for us to need to stop and take a meal. As we gathered over burgers and beer at a roadside hut, one among us raised the possibility that at some moment we had crossed an invisible line separating us from something that had something to do with something which we did not understand. A naïve and drug-addled college student, who appeared to have read a book once, suggested we had passed through a wormhole. Since none of us had seen any worms that might create a hole large enough to drive through, we were instantly skeptical. Despite this she insisted that now we each existed in a series of separate but contiguous dimensions whose only points of convergence were those events which we refused to admit we had witnessed. Taken all together, she talked pretty oddly. And to think of all that money her education must have cost. My wife suspected she was dangerous, but as far as I'm concerned idiocy is only dangerous in the hands of idiots.

Although this woman's suggestion made us uncomfortable, I asked my wife why we should bother with the opinion of someone deluded by medication? In response, my wife pointed out that everyone is taking some sort of medication, and who could tell where that might lead? This student was gorgeous, however, so my wife insisted that since she was high on something other than life, this question was now resolved and I should never think about her again. I find much to admire in the perspicacity of my spouse though she has a stern and humorless spirit. But that stern spirit has kept us focused in our search for that which might be both important and true.

It remains unclear whether it was the burgers or the beer or some other thing, but many among us found themselves so uncomfortable that suddenly they needed to leave. Of course as in any awkward social situation, excuses needed to be made. Lawn-mowing and car-washing, along with a myriad of obligations to children; birthday parties, ball games, piano recitals, each was offered on the altar of social propriety. We aren't barbarians after all, or at least not yet, although the urgency of these departures suggested that such a state is not far off. I had no idea how I should to feel about any of that either, and those absent feelings left a void in my understanding.

Desperation to depart on the part of those departing resulted in a squealing of wheels and rooster-tails of dust. My wife and I had to consider the possibility this urgency was the result of an illness-ray or some other sort of toxic alien emanation directed against the success of our expedition. Those few of us who apparently escaped its effects marveled at this display of energetic panic. Could my wife and I somehow have become immunized against these effects due to our having been exposed to it in some past encounter which we did not recall, as in one of our forgotten dreams? And if so, should we regard ourselves as special by some accidental yet cosmic, and therefore permanent and transcendent, exemption? Heady stuff leaving too much to consider. Consternation muddied our reflections; we looked at each other as if we were looking at other than our selves.

Arrival at the potential location of this possible event came upon us like a sped-forward sunset. We were there as if before we had started. Baffled with surprise we sat in our vehicles, ignitions turned off and hoping to catch up to our selves which, due to our infatuation with the unlikely, were condemned to wander, distracted by the least flicker of light, dawdling and fidgeting like restless children. Our selves must have wandered off, at first confident that our discussions must end soon, until they decided to find amusement further afield, so that eventually our feelings had forgotten their way back. My wife suggested that one of those poorly-socialized and more adventurous selves had led the others astray with a promise of startling sights and grand adventures. Such temptations to adventure and danger are exciting but disastrous to undisciplined emotions.

We awaited the return of our selves with unfocused impatience picking at fingernails, pimples, each other. Our selves along with our feelings remained behind us, back there somewhere, making progress yet misdirected and therefore losing ground with every step. My wife and I discussed the possibility of holding hands, at least until our selves rejoined us, but decided its gesture would confuse our absent selves while giving others an improper permission. If our selves snuck up on us unaware, they might not recognize us, palm to palm and staring vacantly over the dashboard of our consciousness, dizzy with disorientation, stuffy with latent and unacknowledged anguish. In this circumstance our confused selves might move on, certain we must be somewhere still further ahead. And then they would be condemned to continue their search attacked and ravaged by sensations of abandonment and that grief which must result. So she and I sat, each of us with our own hands folded into our own laps, conscious of the possibly of being observed by our lost selves confused and frantic with distress.

The stony and arid plain beyond our windshield was like an invitation to sleep. Even its sky was as flat and uninteresting as a gray concrete sidewalk. Each portion of that vista became a feature since nothing was a feature. It was such a flat and undistinguished terrain that orientation within it was impossible. We yearned for unevenness, for the slightest undulant disturbance, for any variation of elevation or texture or tonality; anything which might be mistaken for singular and at least provide us a point of departure. With such a marker, at least we'd know where we'd been and even how long ago that was.

But my wife and I were without those selves which occupied no specific place and so could only be everywhere at once.

At first she and I mused. This occurrence, whatever it had been, had denatured and drained the material world for as far as our eyes could see. We stood at the edge of a colorless present and featureless future. Whatever was about to happen had the flavor of gruel. On our side of this barrier which kept nothing either in or out, grass and rocks and bugs and sandwich wrappers; on that other side, only gray and coarse sand. Our world remained solid and substantial, while beyond our perimeter everything was indistinguishable from itself. Lacking significant evidence, speculation becomes rampant and frantic. Yet no speculation accounted for what we found around us, if it was indeed around us, and we could not even guess what that might be.

Head-scratching became epidemic. Pointing, ambling in small circles, kicking at the ground with the toe; every analytical tool at our disposal was put to use. Murmuring became talking, which inevitably escalated into shouting whose import made less sense the louder it became. These vocalizations included, but were not limited to, the question of why, and that question hung in the air like an apple without its tree. Eventually some among us insisted there was nothing to see, nothing to do, and so if there was a danger, we were unaware of its nature and therefore powerless against it, whatever it might be. This being the case, they insisted we needed to depart since remaining was no longer useful even as a gesture.

Those urging that we remain claimed the authority of their intuitions. They insisted there were others still out there although we could not see them, perhaps even close by, and we needed to discover who they were and why they needed to kill us. They insisted further that those others continued to watch us, observing and making notes about us for some unknown purpose but which must end with our deaths. And even more frightening, whatever these creatures learned could be used to brutalize our lost selves. Challenged for the absence of evidence, they responded that a continuing presence could be sensed, and intuition of that presence was all the evidence needed. According to them, our invisible visitors had not yet departed; they lurked along the periphery of our eyesight determined to dance within every blind-spot. They insisted the visitors' continued presence indicates their determination to complete a mission obscure to us but profound nonetheless, especially since it must result in our deaths.

Those of us eager to leave were hopeful that none of this could be true. We further agreed that even if they had been present, they must be long-gone by now, especially since we'd failed to give them any reason to remain. These visitors had ended their visit, we insisted, and had returned to wherever they had come from, if they had come from anywhere.

Though vigorous, this disagreement continued but to no result. The rest of us were certain that the insistence on the continuing presence of these visitors was simply an exercise in self-importance. Those insisting on that continuing presence merely cloaked themselves in a fraudulent mystery hopeful of raising their own status within the village. My wife and I assumed that our neighbors had become enamored with the attention of a desperate local media whose representatives, eager to fill empty newspaper space, had accompanied us.

Our arguments over all of this went on and none of us seemed ready to concede even the most minor point.

Fortunately the mayor, her deputy and the police chief had other things on their minds which gave them other things to do and they were eager to get to them, to the distress of all of us.

But those demanding we remain were resourceful, even if delusional. They insisted that, as elected officials, our dignitaries were obliged to remain until this threat to our community was resolved. In response to the assertion that no threat existed, they repeated that an invisible threat remained a threat regardless of its invisibility, and therefore the responsibilities of public officials, though also invisible, remained as well. But finally both sides were compelled to recognize that an impasse had been reached. This left my wife and me in a pleasant quandary. Either I would remain with my wife, or she would depart with me; but in either case at least we would not proceed separately. Although unlikely, there was, I confess, a peculiar yet reassuring uncertainty in all of this. Remain or depart; our status as a couple was assured, and our collaboration, in turn, would likely follow. My wife's speculation about all of this remained as baffling and obscure as ever.

And yet I struggled in my consternation. If we had been visited by visitors, who might they have been and what had been the purpose of their visit? These questions bedeviled all of us although apparently me most of all. But my wife trumped every question with one of her own: since so many of us remained unconvinced by the lack of evidence, what, she asked, would count as evidence?

I explained earlier that my wife is one really smart individual, but it should come as no surprise that I endure ambivalence on that issue. As smart as she is, she is wrong remarkably often. Thus, my response to her question was a silence which answered every question.

Meanwhile, despite the amount of time that had passed, our selves remained lost, and I came to suspect even more lost than before. So my wife and I confronted a more urgent difficulty, although one neither of us was equipped to resolve. By leaving, we were compelled to assume our selves, although unaided, still would manage to find us.

Those determined to remain were forced to concede that if these visitors were waiting for something, we had no idea what it was or even if we would recognize it when we saw it. So finally the question was asked: could there be any defense against a non-existent threat? My wife, I am embarrassed to report, was among the last to concede that only nothing comes from nothing. I've always admired her determination but not so very much that particular evening.

When all of us finally returned to our vehicles we discovered that the mayor, the sheriff and her deputy had become so thoroughly entangled they could only be pried apart with a length of metal pipe. This demanded effort as well as time and so we did not reach our home until very late.

My wife and I sat in chairs in our living room opposite each other panting as if we'd just run miles and hopeful that soon our feelings would find us. We did not stare at each other, but neither could we turn completely away. We did not ignore each other, but neither did we maintain eye-contact for more than an instant. Even our labored breathing, though it demanded effort, only just broke our silence. From time to time I glanced at the clock on the mantel. But I did not become seriously concerned until I caught my wife sneaking looks at the clock as well. Finally we needed to admit that the arrival of our feelings was long-delayed and it was now appropriate for us to worry.

This was not the first time we had experienced such confusion. But on previous occasions our confusion had lasted only for brief periods of time, and our feelings had never gone so far astray or for so long. So our vigil tested our patience for our feelings as well as our loyalty to each other. Our feelings, after all, knew how much we depended on them. They understood that without them, moments became invisible to us, or worse, frozen in place. We had returned to our home, although as unlikely captives, while our feelings remained out there, somewhere, their delirious paths more circuitous than either of us could imagine, and perhaps even more convoluted than they could imagine. Powerless to force their return, we assumed that inevitably they would arrive from whatever they'd gotten themselves up to. We waited in silence. This exercise was a lot like watching a bathtub fill that has a hole in its bottom.

Eventually my wife and I gave up and we had already gone to bed when our feelings returned. We listened as the front door opened and then closed, listened to muttering and quiet laughter as they climbed the stairs and followed the hallway but then hesitated at our bedroom door. We did not glance at the clock though we could roughly guess the hour. It took another moment before our selves gathered their courage and entered our room and then climbed into the bed beside us. Which, unsurprisingly, is when the trouble began.

First there was squirming and the tugging at blankets. Then came jabbing and giggling. My wife and I attempted to ignore all of this, and managed to do so for some time. But inevitably someone's feelings got hurt and then things became turbulent.

Up out of the bed, on with the light, this must stop, or so my wife announced. At first our feelings laid there insisting they would rest now, it had been a long day and they were tired. But as always, her determination overwhelmed every compromise. When she demanded to know where they had been, they said nowhere, and when she asked what they had done, they said nothing. Adopting a more pointed tact, she asked what had caused them to become lost and to arrive home late. Didn't they know we would be waiting up for them? Didn't they understand that we tortured ourselves with worry about them? Adopting angelic postures, our feelings instantly feigned sleep.

Around this time I noticed our bedroom beginning to fill with bemusement. This was immediately followed by an in-flow of consternation. There had been a sequence of events which needed to be sorted through, like an old and unopened box stumbled upon in an attic. It could not be tossed aside without an examination of its contents. Someone had made an effort to pack that metaphorical box, and so must have hoped to preserve whatever was inside. And just so with our visitation; someone somewhere intended that we recognize something or become convinced of something. But our feelings had failed to cooperate or even become engaged, and worse, they now refused to acknowledge let alone regret our distress.

With retreat into sleep hopeless, we tramped as a group down to the kitchen where over coffee we discussed just how important the contribution of feelings were to our aspiration to understand this world and what happens within it. This world can only be recognized by how we feel about it. My wife insisted that the material world was not immediately obvious and self-explanatory, and so we needed to employ our interpretive faculties, which included our feelings, in order to stimulate and coordinate our imaginations. At the end of this explanation I was tempted to assume she had won, although I'd missed exactly how she'd done it.

But in the silence that followed, we listened to our feelings snore as loud as pick-up trucks. I was relieved in an odd way when finally our feelings fell asleep.

I raised the possibility to my wife that awakening those feelings and interrogating them further could only open old and very dark passages which would lead to even darker places. But she shrugged with indifference, insisting that there wasn't anything we could find that we couldn't resolve. Besides, our visitation must possess some significance, and that simple fact can't be dismissed. So even at the risk of releasing some phantom from the past or some preview of our inaccessible future, my wife insisted we needed to know what our feelings knew, needed to see what they had seen and just the way they had seen it. But by then I discovered that my attention had wandered off and refused to be found. My wife was unimpressed.

We returned to the bedroom and to our snoring feelings, brought out blankets and pillows from the closet, retreated to the living-room and tossed them in the middle of the floor, and there we made love of a sort. Afterward, we slept separately on the two couches.

Neither of us could have returned to the bedroom. We could never have slept through all of that snoring or the bewildering jungle of unresolved ambiguities or even that distracted consternation and complacency which all of this implied, an indifference toward ignorance and the bittersweet vacuity of emotions.

A.W. DEANNUNTIS lives in Philadelphia, Pennsylvania and has published fiction in more than twenty periodicals that include *The Evansville Review, Philadelphia Short Stories, Silent Voices, The Armchair Aesthete, Timber Creek Review, Lynx Eye, Los Angeles Review, Mind in Motion* (Pushcart Prize nomination), *Kiosk, Cimarron Review, California Quarterly, Dog River Review* and *Coe Review*, as well as the novels *Master Siger's Dream* and *The Mermaid at the Americana Arms Motel* and the short-story collection *The Final Death of Rock-and-Roll and Other Stories* with What Books Press.

TITLES FROM
WHAT BOOKS PRESS

POETRY

Molly Bendall & Gail Wronsky, *Bling & Fringe (The L.A. Poems)*

Laurie Blauner, *It Looks Worse Than I Am*

Kevin Cantwell, *One of Those Russian Novels*

Ramón García, *Other Countries*

Karen Kevorkian, *Lizard Dream*

Holaday Mason & Sarah Maclay, *The "She" Series: A Venice Correspondence*

Carolie Parker, *Mirage Industry*

Patty Seyburn, *Perfecta*

Judith Taylor, *Sex Libris*

Lynne Thompson, *Start with a Small Guitar*

Gail Wronsky, *So Quick Bright Things*
BILINGUAL, SPANISH TRANSLATED BY ALICIA PARTNOY

ART

Gronk, *A Giant Claw*
BILINGUAL, SPANISH

Chuck Rosenthal, Gail Wronsky & Gronk,
Tomorrow You'll Be One of Us: Sci Fi Poems

PROSE

Rebbecca Brown, *They Become Her*

François Camoin, *April, May, and So On*

A.W. DeAnnuntis, *Master Siger's Dream*

A.W. DeAnnuntis, *The Final Death of Rock and Roll and Other Stories*

A.W. DeAnnuntis, *The Mermaid at the Americana Arms Motel*

A.W. DeAnnuntis, *The Mysterious Islands and Other Stories*

Katharine Haake, *The Origin of Stars and Other Stories*

Katharine Haake, *The Time of Quarantine*

Mona Houghton, *Frottage & Even As We Speak: Two Novellas*

Rich Ives, *The Balloon Containing the Water Containing the Narrative Begins Leaking*

Rod Val Moore, *Brittle Star*

Annette Leddy, *Earth Still*

Chuck Rosenthal, *Are We Not There Yet? Travels in Nepal, North India, and Bhutan*

Chuck Rosenthal, *Coyote O'Donohughe's History of Texas*

Chuck Rosenthal, *West of Eden: A Life in 21st Century Los Angeles*

Chuck Rosenthal & Gail Wronsky, *The Shortest Fairwells are the Best*

What Books Press books may be ordered from:

SPDBOOKS.ORG | ORDERS@SPDBOOKS.ORG | (800) 869 7553 | AMAZON.COM

Visit our website at

WHATBOOKSPRESS.COM

Printed in the USA
CPSIA information can be obtained
at www.ICGtesting.com
LVHW041344191023
761544LV00004B/410